A Prophecy to Unveil

Sara Kohan

Dedications

To my friend, Reagan, who kept me accountable while writing it.

I miss our weekly work sessions.

Querencia
Island of Harnew
Cavern Cliffs
Town of Ayward
Linnea Kingdom

Erontil Mountains
Claude's Cottage
Malgion Mountains

PRONUNCIATION GUIDE

CHARACTERS

Adira: ah-die-ra

Soren: sore-in

Poderosa: pod-er-osa

Esper: esp-er

Conri: con-ree

Cain: cane

Fadama: fad-ama

Wilhema: will-hema

Tatsuya: tat-soo-ya

Tiamat: tee-ah-mat

Eira: air-ah

Saline: s-ah-leen

Atin: at-in

Dahak: duh-hawk

PLACES

Celestara: celeste-are-a

Enelon: en-el-on

Modereo: mod-air-io

Linnea: lin-ay-ah

Querencia: quer-en-cee-ah

Noelani: no-lawn-ee

OTHERS

Stregone (masc.): stray-gone-ay

Stregona (fem): stray-gone-ah

Stregoni (plu.): stray-gone-ee

Enid: ah-nid

Makutu: mah-coo-too

Astraia: ah-stray-ah

Vormr: vore-mr

Umbrai: um-brigh

Invicta: in-vick-ta

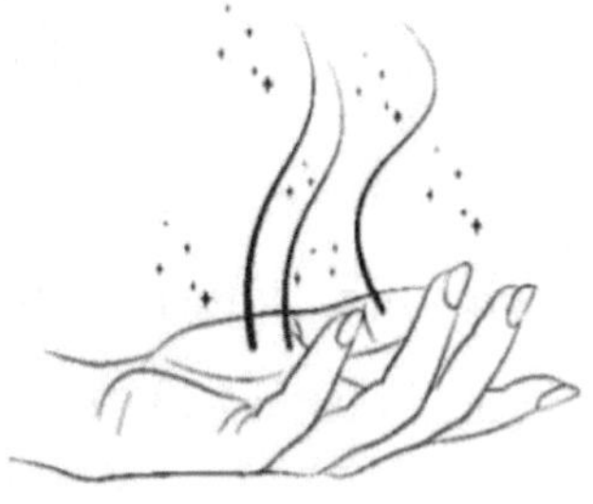

Chapter 1

The dark passage looms in front of me as I run. Growls bounce off the walls as I turn the corner. A sickening thud echoes as one of the beasts miscalculates the turn, its claws scraping against stone. At the end of the hall, a crack of light beckons me forward. I risk a glance behind, and a sliver of fear curls up my spine as I see the Umbrai gaining on me. I just have to make it to the stone door. My heart pulses frantically in my chest, almost drowning out the sound of their sharp claws pounding against the hard floor. The harsh sound gets louder and louder, carrying my heartrate with it.

One of the creatures lashes out with a sharp claw, and I feel my jacket rip. A scream escapes me as my blood boils from the sting of the fresh wound. My jaw clenches against the pain, I push myself faster. Seconds later, I burst through the door of the secret passage. I dig my heels into the ground as I turn sharply. Throwing all my weight against the heavy stone, I shove it closed. It clicks shut just as the Umbrai slam into it from the other side.

I stumble backward and land with a jarring thud onto the ground outside the palace. Gritting my teeth, I push myself up and head towards the forest. The sting of the open wound burns my back, turning my breath labored. Panic claws at my chest as I hear the guards shouting. I don't let myself freeze with fear. Instead, I clear my mind and focus on the training my body already knows by heart.

King Dahak will be looking for me now. The entire castle will be on high alert. After all, I don't belong in this realm. Even now, the air in Enelon feels heavier, different from Modereo's magic-rich lands. A reminder that I don't belong here. It is forbidden to travel between realms, so naturally, I'm being hunted.

A low snarl echoes near the edge of the castle walls. I whip my head around at the sound, my long brown hair smacking the side of my face with the motion. Thankfully, the Umbrai don't seem able to pass the castle wards. They prowl forward, their hunched forms rippling with barely-contained aggression. Their fur, slick with sweat and filth, smells of rotting meat. Red eyes glow like embers, locking onto me with hunger. They are usually wild and uncontrollable. Yet somehow, King Dahak has managed to control them and has them guarding the grounds. They are incredibly stubborn creatures, so they must be bound by the same wards that keep others out.

My hand instinctively reaches for my pendant, reminding me of my training, grounding me. My mother gave it to me when I was young. The engraved symbol on it represents strength and power, mirroring the meaning of my name—Adira. I picture her piercing blue eyes and the displeased look she'd give if she knew I'd gotten injured. I internally roll my own green eyes at the thought but feel a renewed sense of determination.

Pushing off the tree I was leaning against, I keep moving. A branch snags at my shirt, tearing a piece off. I let it flutter to the ground while I focus on my breathing. A sharp hiss escapes my lips and I fall to my knees as a new wave of pain flares through me.

I take a few deep breaths, forcing the blackness out of my vision. *I guess the adrenaline has worn off,* I think to myself.

Shaking off the dizziness, I grab a handful of dirt and rub it all over myself, masking my scent as best as I can. I rip a large strip from my already ruined shirt and press it against the wound on my back. The blood makes it stick in place. Looking down at my filthy clothes, I know I might regret this later, but I can't risk leaving a trail to track. Swaying slightly, I push myself back to my feet and shake my head to clear the dizziness.

I glance around. The dense forest stretches endlessly before me. I decide that my best chance is to stick close to the shoreline. Turning toward the moss-laden trees, which seem to press in on me as I push forward.

I walk for what feels like miles before stumbling upon a cave. I peer into the entrance, but the only thing I can discern is that it's damp, not to mention dark. My nose wrinkles in distaste. Squinting into the darkness, I notice the shadows shifting unnaturally. I scan my surroundings for an alternative, but exhaustion wins. I slip through the cave's wide mouth, coldness seeping into me the farther I go. I venture deeper in than most would dare go in fear of the Invicta. They are creatures said to lurk in the shadows, waiting for weary travelers to wander in to rest—before devouring their souls.

First, they immobilize you. They feed off fear, so the more you struggle, the more they enjoy it. They are complex and insidious, dragging forth your worst memories, ensnaring you in your own mind. As you're lost in your nightmares, they creep closer, their shadows slipping into your mind and chest, draining your soul until there's nothing left but an empty vessel.

But considering an entire kingdom of guards is chasing me, I'll take my chances with the Invicta.

I walk to the back of the cave **and settle in for the night.**

***

I awake when it's still dark out and am uncertain why. I open my eyes, feeling the press of cold steel at my throat.

I swallow shallowly. "Hello, boys." Blinking into the darkness, I find myself surrounded by guards, their swords glinting in the dim light. My breath hitches.

Forcing a smirk, I say, "Took you long enough to find me."

"Shut up," one of them hisses. "Get up, filth. His Majesty has plans for you."

A manic smile crosses his face. I suppress as shiver.

"Now, now, that's not very polite." I tilt my head. "Did you really think I wouldn't be prepared for your arrival?" I say, smirking.

They look at each other somewhat nervously.

I shift slightly, casting a look over my shoulder towards the darkness of the cave. The guards notice the movement and instinctively draw back from me.

"As promised," I say smoothly, "your snack."

Their faces drain of color as I stand and slink towards the entrance of the cave.

They all turn pale as the shadows begin to move. Panic erupts among them as they scramble to flee. But it's too late. A chorus of screams fills the cavern.

There is one thing most people always seem to forget about the Invicta—that they can be bargained with. I only had to promise it my soul if I failed to deliver five others. Risky? Perhaps. Stupid? Most definitely. But it paid off.

A thread of guilt runs through me as I look at the thrashing bodies of the five guards. Shadows move in and out of them as they struggle. *They were only acting on the King's orders...but they did try to kill me.* I tell myself. But as I stare down at them, I know their haunted expressions would torment me in the nights to come.

My mother's voice echoes in my mind: *There is no room in this world for weakness.*

As soon as the screams die down and the shadows have receded, I step back into the cave and see the guards spread out on the cold cavern floor, their vacant eyes staring into nothingness. A few of them had pissed themselves with fear, ruining their once-pristine blue uniforms.

I quickly grab a sword from one of the dead guards and slip back into the trees before the Invicta changes its mind about sparing me.

I head toward the only person in this realm who might welcome me.

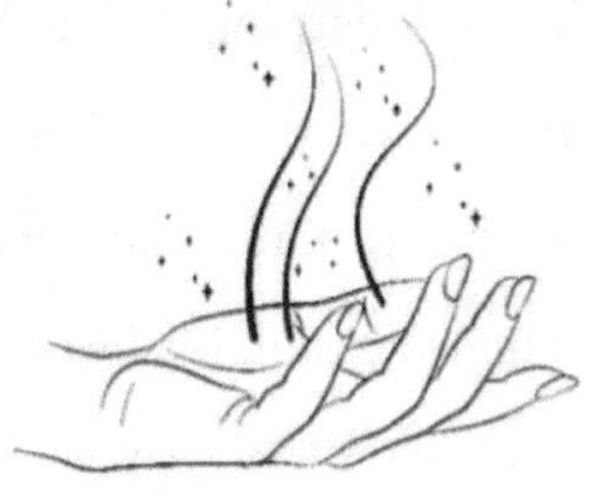

Chapter 2

After almost a day of walking, I feel my strength returning. I pluck a handful of berries from a low-hanging bush, popping them into my mouth. A faint tingling spreads through my fingertips. My magic is returning. *Finally.* Being cut off from it for so long left me feeling hollow, like a part of me was missing. King Dahak had kept it subdued with all the drugs they forced into my system while I was imprisoned. I shiver as an ache spreads through my body. But the disorienting feeling is already starting to fade the longer I'm exposed to the elements.

In Modereo, the way of life is almost completely opposite to this realm. Here, they have cold, long winters that isolate the humans who live here, whereas we have temperate conditions that allow us to access our magic more easily. Luckily, I arrived during the four months when it's not unbearable here. Not to mention, magic is almost nonexistent in Enelon. King Dahak punishes all who show control over the elements. In Enelon, you also won't find any females that are part of the guard, whereas in Modereo, we are trained alongside the men.

This is why, when I hear a branch crack in the distance, I don't panic. Instead, I drop into my fighting stance. Making my steps silent, I creep forward and peer into the clearing of trees. My stomach clenches. Soren. Of all the hunters in Enelon, it had to be him. Tension fills me at the thought of fighting him. My heartbeat picks up, thumping erratically in my chest. I slowly back away without taking my eyes off him—which, as it turns out, isn't the best idea, considering I can't see where I'm going.

I cringe as my foot cracks the smallest branch. Soren's head snaps toward me. We lock eyes for a second before I turn and run. I push myself harder as I hear him crashing through the trees behind me. I summon my power and let it flow to the surface. I picture a root snapping up and grabbing Soren's foot. I release my magic and hear him grunt in surprise. A thud follows, but I don't stop to make sure he stays down. Adrenaline surges through me as I run away. I swiftly melt deeper into the trees, using them for cover as I reach the cliff's edge.

A familiar feeling flows through me as I recognize the area. When the Arae split the world in two, it created identical cliffsides where the world ripped. I go left and push aside the branches to find the overgrown pathway down. In Modereo, this path is well known and used to take us down to a cave by the water. The cave is used by Stregoni to replenish their magic. When the moon is high, it passes over the top of the open cave and strengthens the magic wielder inside.

I reach the entrance and listen for any sign of Soren. Turning to the cave, I see that it's empty. *Thank goddess for small miracles.* I start to twist back to the opening, and a flash of yellow catches my eye. Leaning in closer, I notice a small yellow symbol inked on the wall. Not recognizing it, I shrug it off, focusing on my plan.

I summon up the slight bit of magic I have, building a trap. If anyone crosses through the entrance, a wave of water will come from the ocean, surrounding the intruder and dragging them into the water. *That should give me enough time.* I think to myself, satisfyingly. I settle against one of the hard walls, fatigue rapidly melting into me from my use of magic. *Not to mention being chased by this realm's favored assassin.*

The fading sun against the calm water lulls me into a relaxed state. I stay awake for as long as I can, but I eventually drift off.

***

The sound of sloshing liquid wakes me. Disoriented, I blink away the fog, quickly getting ahold of my surroundings. *Right. The trap. Soren.*

I push myself up, my body shakes with pain. Gritting my teeth, I ignore my fatigue, snatching up the sword on the ground. Turning to the opening, I see Soren lifting himself up from the water.

I smirk to myself. *At least the trap worked.*

He smoothly unsheathes his sword, stepping closer to me.

"Soren. Of course. I thought I lost you."

He seems surprised at the sound of his name on my tongue.

He quickly wipes the look away and scowls.

"Lose me? Adira, you should know–I'm impossible to shake."

Feeling my reserve, I notice it's nearly empty. Suppressing a groan, I size up Soren. *On a normal day I'd be able to take him, but right now? I'm so weak, I can barely stand up.*

Panic fills me. *I won't win. But damn if I don't go down without a fight.* My grip tightens against the leather of the pommel.

He reaches into his pocket, pulling out a small oval shaped object. Pressing a button, he tosses it deeper into the cave. Closer to me.

Confusion causes me to freeze. Tilting my head, I think. *What is that?*

A second later, smoke appears from it. Rapidly filling the cave. My nostrils flare as I recognize the scent. *Fucking suppressants. Again.*

I try to race forward, but my legs feel like lead. I sway on my feet, coughing from the unclean air. My mind races for a solution. Pressure fills my head before I can grasp a solid idea. Falling to the side, I look toward the entrance. Through the smoke, I see Soren standing outside, smirking at me. His smug face is the last thing I see.

***

When I wake up, my hands are tied behind my back. My eyes flutter open, and I blink, trying to clear my head. I can feel the drugs suppressing my magic just below the surface of my skin. I try to wriggle out of the ties.

"Good luck getting out of those, Adira," a voice says from the dark left corner of the cave. I slump back against the wall, feeling drained from being cut off from my magic.

Shaking my head to clear the mental fog, I turn toward the voice. Soren steps into the light, smirking at my failed attempt to escape.

I bite my tongue. Refusing to acknowledge that I was bested.

"Nothing to say?" he taunts.

I open my mouth to retort, but he cuts me off.

"Now, here's how this is going to go. I'm going to ask you some questions, and you're going to answer them without being difficult. Alright? Think you can do that?" he smirks condescendingly.

"Does wearing the King's leash make you feel powerful? Let me clue you in on something: killing people still means you end a life. You're a monster," I spit out.

"It's called justice, princess. Killing criminals is what keeps this kingdom running."

My lip curls in annoyance at the pet name.

"Says who? Your precious King? At least my King doesn't kill innocent people."

I think.

He scoffs, not seeming to believe me. "Then why did you come to our realm?"

I pause, unsure how much to tell him. *It doesn't matter if he kills me,* I tell myself. So, I divulge the truth.

"Modereo is dying. A Vormr is spreading through the land. It initially started in your realm, so I crossed over and traced it back to the castle. I was investigating when I got caught and was sent to prison until the King had time to question me. I managed to escape and, well, you know the rest."

Soren stares at me silently, probably gauging whether to believe me or not.

"You don't have to believe me, but either way, it's the truth," I say as I lean back against the cave wall. But I hope he does believe me. *It would be such a waste to die at the mere age of twenty-four*, I think to myself bitterly.

"Of course, I don't believe you. What even is a Vormr? It sounds like something you made up."

I glance at him dryly. "I didn't make it up. It's an affliction that attacks the land. Decaying and withering the terrain. It's twisted magic pulls from the earth, draining it. Therefore, Stregoni are finding it harder to wield the elements. As it eats through the land, it gets stronger and spreads."

"What would Enelon have to do with poisoning your land?" He asks, disbelief apparent in his tone.

"That's what I'm trying to find out. I think it has something to do with your precious King." I admit with a mocking tone.

His jaw twitches.

"Why can't your kind just stop it?"

I sigh.

"If it were that easy, we would. No one's magic has been able to contain it. A few people have tried. The worst was when an earth wielder tried to push back on it, it responded tenfold. Shadows covered the land, turning it desolate. Everyone in that village died."

He shifts slightly on his feet, the only sign of his unease.

I file that away for later and sit up straighter. "So, where are you taking me?"

"Back to the castle, where do you think?"

"I think I can persuade you otherwise, Soren."

"Doubtful." He responds flatly.

Luckily, I know his story. In my realm, we have records on their world as well as ours, so as not to repeat history. The Sage family is the only living bloodline that can recount current events whilst writing, having no prior recollection of them. Soren Banrs was in the books as the youngest assassin to be chosen by the King himself.

Looking at him now, the descriptions did not do him justice. If you search up the definition of tall, dark, and handsome, Soren's picture will come up.

"I know that King Dahak slaughtered your family when you were younger, making you an orphan. How does it feel to serve the man who murdered your family? I can't imagine it feels good."

He lets out a short, pained laugh.

"I have no choice."

His hand twitches to his wrist. My eyes follow the movement and see red ink, twirled into a knot. The symbol of a blood oath.

My breath catches.

"He made you swear a blood oath." I whisper in shock. Wondering how I didn't come to this conclusion myself.

Soren's breathing falters slightly. His eyes glaze over, lost in thought.

"I can help you break it." I tell him confidently.

Shaking his head, he snaps back to the present.

"It's a blood oath, princess. You break it, you die." He scoffs at me.

"But you've never had magic on your side before, have you? Which is where I come in. If you help me solve the problem in my realm, I'll help you break your oath."

He stares at me with an impassive look on his face. "And how do I know you won't run on home after I've helped you?"

"Easy. While we're fixing my problem, I'll start fixing yours as well." I give him a big smile.

His eyes narrow on me. "I won't blindly trust you."

You mean, like I'm blindly trusting you? You could be lying! I shout in my mind, eyeing the mark of the blood oath.

I roll my eyes. "Okay. What would you have me do?"

"Prove yourself."

"How?"

Reaching into his pocket, he pulls out a thin tube filled with swirling purple liquid. Truth serum.

My eyes widen in disbelief. "How do you have that?"

He smirks. "I have my ways."

My heartbeat quickens at the sight of it.

"So, will you take it? Or are you lying about everything?"

I breathe out my unease. "Fine. Bring it over here."

He walks over to me, uncapping the small vial. I tilt my head back and let him drip it into my mouth. Once it's empty, he stands, taking a few steps back.

Awareness spreads through me as it reaches my reserves. It grasps onto my magic and floods my bloodstream. A loose feeling fills me, making me light as air. A giddy grin spreads across my face.

"Ask what you must." I titter out.

"Who are you working for?" He demands.

So boring. I think, rolling my eyes.

"No one. I'm here on my own."

"What's your full name?"

"Adira Selcouth." *That's an easy one.*

"Are you planning to double cross me?"

"No." The answer flows out of me easily.

Some tension leaks out of his shoulders.

"Will your magic be able to break a blood oath?"

I hesitate a moment.

"No. But with the help of my magic, I'm certain we can figure it out."

"What is your plan?"

"We'll start by sneaking back into the castle. There's a book that can help the both of us."

He sits there contemplating if my offer is genuine.

My mind starts to clear, the last of the truth serum fading from my body. After what feels like an hour, he finally, albeit reluctantly, says, "Okay, deal. I'll work with you. But if you screw me over, I'll bring your head to the King myself."

Victorious, I smile. "I'd expect nothing less."

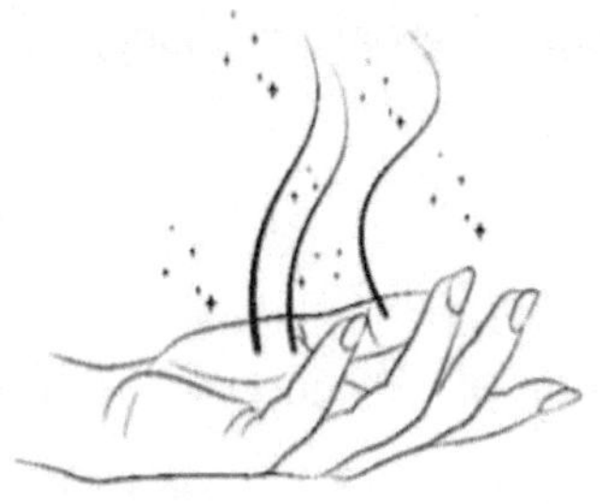

Chapter 3

The next day, we head back in the direction of the kingdom, giving the castle walls a wide berth. I walk ahead, feeling Soren glaring daggers into my back, as if he can't believe he's trusting me.

Without turning around, I say, "You know, if you don't trust me, we won't get very far."

"Of course I don't trust you," he replies without skipping a beat.

"Okay, that's fair, but you can at least talk to me. We don't have to walk in uncomfortable silence."

He ignores me.

I try again. "So, what do you like to do besides kill people?"

I can feel him scowling at my back when he says, "I don't like to kill people, but I have to."

"Do you really?"

"Yes. It's either that or I'm dead," he retorts, as if it's obvious.

"Hmm, okay. So how do you decide that your life is better than theirs?" I ask, throwing him a look over my shoulder.

His already stony face clouds over as he shoots me a glower, turning away in silence. Mentally, I groan, realizing he won't say anything for the rest of the day.

***

The sun is almost completely gone when he says we should stop for the night. I don't argue. We find an open area between the trees. We are only about a day's walk from the palace, so we decide against a fire.

I use my magic to heat the ground around us to a more bearable temperature. He grunts in acknowledgment. *I'll take that as a thank you.*

"I'll take first watch," Soren says, already settling against a tree.

I shrug. "Okay, wake me when it's my turn."

I shift my body, nestling myself into the warm ground. I stay awake for a while, thinking about Soren changing his mind and deciding to kill me. Every slight shuffle he makes tenses me up, preparing for an attack. After what feels like hours, I force myself to relax and eventually drift off to sleep.

Sometime later, I'm abruptly woken.

Groggily, I ask, "Is it my turn for wat—"

"Shh," he whispers harshly. "There's something here."

I then notice that half of his body is covering mine. I flush despite the cool air. Shifting my weight, I push him off. He blinks, realizing he was on top of me.

I grab my knife from the sheath on my right thigh and do a wide scan of the area. I pull my magic to the surface and find it's still weakened, so I decide to call upon the easiest element: earth.

Crouching down, I plant my left hand in the soil. Closing my eyes, I call upon my magic once more. I channel through the forest and sense two men coming towards us from the north.

"Two. Coming from the north," I say quietly, opening my eyes.

He swings to the left, and we slowly creep forward, making no noise. I let my magic hum back to the surface of my skin and will some roots to grab the men's ankles, giving us an unnecessary but welcome advantage.

"Shit, the little witch," we hear one of them grunt.

Soren looks back at me questioningly, and I just lift a shoulder and smirk.

We step into the clearing where the men are struggling to free their ankles from the roots. When they see us, they grab their fallen swords and point them at us. A valiant effort.

Surprisingly enough, they aren't soldiers from Linnea, Soren's kingdom.

"Who are you working for, and why are you hunting the witch?" Soren interrogates, pressing a sword to one of the soldier's throats.

"Hey," I scoff at the word witch. "We prefer to be called Stregoni."

They all ignore me. *Typical men.*

I take in their forest green uniforms and note the yellow axe sewn onto their right sleeves. A wave of recognition flows through me. I wade through my foggy, drugged memories and remember the same symbol on the cave wall.

"We are Enid, the rebellion. And you will never kill us all," one spits at our feet.

"Who are you rebelling?"

"We rebel all evil beings." The big one says vaguely.

My nose wrinkles in confusion.

"And how do you know who is evil?"

"The Divinità tells us." He says smugly.

The other soldier snaps his head towards his companion. "Shut up, Tucker. No information can be shared, you big oaf."

They glance at each other for a silent moment, then both nod. The big one, Tucker, hesitates. The smaller man whispers to himself. "*Tolle me nunc.*"

He slams his body to the right, ramming his hand into a sharp rock. It breaks his skin. Blood drips from the wound. As soon as it hits the ground, he starts convulsing and dies. Soren shoots forward, grabbing Tucker's jaw before he can do the same.

"Nice try, big guy."

Soren locks Tucker's arms behind him. Securing him.

I squat down next to Tucker.

"Okay, Tucker. How come I've never heard of Enid?"

He hesitates. I call my magic up to the surface, letting it flicker into my eyes. The clearing takes on a whiteish hue.

Fear shines in his eyes.

"The Divinità protects us." He sputters out. I let my power slip back inside me. My vision turns back to normal.

"Who is the Divinità?"

"I don't know. Only a few soldiers know him. He tells his plans to those soldiers and they in turn, tell us."

My eyebrows raise.

"And you just blindly follow this person?"

Tucker shrugs. "It's better than being under Dahak's rule. The Divinità supplies food and shelter for those who pledge their allegiance."

"What plan are you following right now?" Soren asks.

Tucker falters. His features harden.

"Why should I tell you? You are going to kill me anyway."

My lips twitch at his tone, *look who's finally grown a pair.*

"Come on." I tease. "Tell us something interesting. Something other than this mysterious being you blindly follow."

Tucker glares at me.

Soren speaks up.

"There are things worse than death." He says with a menacing tone.

Tucker swallows hard, his face filled with dread.

"Tolle me nunc. Compromissum." He whispers quickly.

His face twists in pain. Bloodshot eyes lock onto mine. He coughs and blood spurts out. I leap back to avoid the spray. Soren releases him and he immediately doubles over, grabbing his stomach. He falls on his side, wheezing. Then, he twitches and stops. Unseeing eyes stare at the sky.

"Dammit, there was two phrases. Well, that was a bust," I say nonchalantly with a shrug.

Soren looks at me like I've grown two heads.

I look around for an Invicta to be slinking around, but the forest is quiet.

"What?"

"Wouldn't have pegged you for the 'who cares about their lives' type of person," Soren says.

"Well, when they are trying to kill me, I have very little sympathy for them," I reply.

My mind drifts back to all the dead bodies I've seen. All the ones that have died by my hand or my actions. I swallow the rising remorse, pushing the bloody images out of my thoughts.

He stares at me for a moment. "You're not responsible for their deaths. Or any that you've had to kill in self-defense."

I tilt my head at his response. Almost like he pulled my thoughts right out of my head.

"In the end, it doesn't matter. Dead is dead."

"I guess so." He agrees slowly, dropping the subject. Then he tilts his head up to the sky.

"We might as well start walking now; it's almost dawn."

I glance up. "You let me sleep longer than your share of the watch. Why?"

He shrugs. "I wasn't tired."

I'm really starting to hate those shrugs.

"Plus, I don't trust you not to try and escape while I'm sleeping," he continues with a pointed gaze at me.

I roll my eyes.

"It goes both ways, pretty boy. I thought you were going to decide this truce wasn't worth it and finish me off while I slept."

Now he rolls his eyes.

"If I wanted to kill you, I wouldn't need to wait until you were asleep," he states cockily, choosing to ignore the insulting nickname.

"So confident," I tease in a serious tone.

He just casually shrugs again. I bite my lip in annoyance at the gesture.

"Maybe we should test that out?" I challenge, stopping in a clearing.

He stops and turns. "Maybe we should." Soren agrees, putting his pack down.

"What are the ground rules? No magic? No weapons?" I ask, putting my own pack down.

He immediately scoffs.

"You maybe had a chance with weapons, but there is no way you will best me in a hand-to-hand fight."

I just raise an eyebrow. This isn't the first time I've heard this comment from a man. It's my absolute least favorite thing when a man thinks he can beat you just because he's, well, a man. After hearing it so many times growing up, I made sure I spent extra time training with all kinds of people and all kinds of weapons.

"Well," he urges, "are we doing this?"

Anticipation fills me, and I try to hide my smile.

"Absolutely," I reply.

I get into my fighting stance and assess him. As we circle each other, I must admit, it's hard to find any apparent weaknesses. I decide to let him attack me first.

He shoots forward, and I shift back onto my right foot, pushing him sideways as I do. His punch doesn't land as he skirts past me. I see a flash of surprise on his face, followed by a scowl. He comes forward again, feigning left but going right. I brace myself as he lands a punch on the left side of my temple. My head snaps to the side, but I quickly recover, whipping back my head and my fist. I land a punch at the bottom of his ribcage and bounce back from him—though not quickly enough, as he gets a solid kick into my left side.

I hiss at the pain and stumble a bit but swiftly get back into my stance. This time, I go on the offensive and nimbly block his first retaliatory punch. I get solid contact with his left cheek, his head turns from the impact. I don't waste any time as I step forward around his body with my left foot and spin back with my elbow. It connects with his back. I ignore the sharp pain that ricochets up my arm from the contact.

He twists around and grabs me from behind, holding me against his broad chest, locking my arms in front of my body.

"Hmm, ready to give up yet?" Soren's voice brags from behind me.

I don't say anything but relax slightly in his hold. He loosens his grip, no doubt thinking he's won. When I can move my arms, I whip them down to my sides fast, breaking the hold. I bring my fist back and smash his nose. His hand automatically goes up to it. I grab his other arm and shift my body weight, using it to fling him over my shoulder and onto the ground. I quickly straddle him and pin down his arms.

With a smirk, I repeat his words back to him, "Are you ready to give up yet?"

He overpowers me and flips us around. I grunt at the impact and struggle against his calloused hands. But it's no use with his weight on top of me.

"I have to say, princess, that was quite impressive," he murmurs darkly.

"Whatever," I scoff back. "I still lost."

My mother's face of disappointment flashes through my mind, and my face scrunches with an echo of guilt. Of course, she's gone and can still make me feel less than.

Soren stares at me for a moment before speaking.

"If you didn't try to keep me pinned down at the end, you could have had me. Since I'm bigger, the best chance is for you to knock your opponent out," he offers.

"I don't need your advice. I do just fine on my own," I sniff, lifting my chin up.

He releases his hold on me and gets up.

"Whatever you say, princess."

I push to my feet and try to ignore the stinging in my side. *That's going to bruise,* I think as I wince to myself.

Soren has a hard look on his face as he notices me wincing.

"I don't know what your problem is. But we should get moving," I grumble, picking up my pack.

He wordlessly picks up his pack, and we start walking.

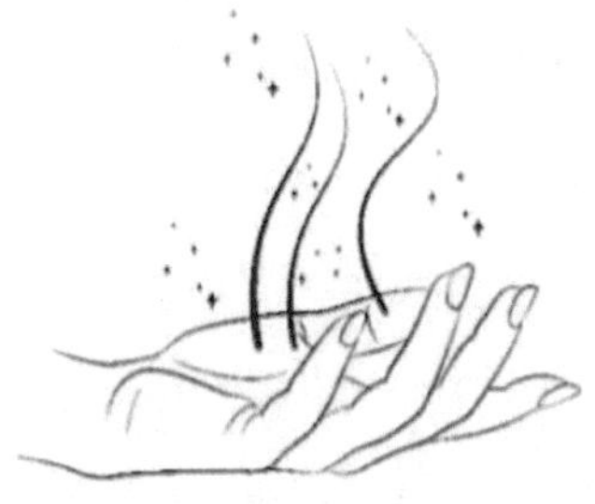

Chapter 4

We are about half a day's walk from the castle when Soren asks me what the plan is to get inside. *It's about time. I'm surprised he waited this long.* I think warily, suspicion gnawing at me.

"Magic," I reply, knowing the one-worded response will irritate him.

He grits his teeth and tries again. "What magic do you have?"

I think about how much I want to tell him. In both realms, La Scelta is held. It is a choosing ceremony where one's powers are revealed. The ceremony in Modereo is sacred, while in Enelon it's feared, as King Dahak kills any who show signs of power if they do not submit to his mind enslavement.

It is common for most magic wielders to have control over one or two elements. It is uncommon for some to have control over three. It's very rare to have control over four.

My thoughts drag me back to the first ceremony I saw.

I had just turned eleven and my mother thought it would be a good idea to observe one. As we walk to the temple, she turns to me.

"I need you to pay attention today." She sternly tells me.

"Okay." I agree, confused.

We make it to the white stone building. Tall pillars line the front entrance. Stepping through, I feel like a princess walking into her castle. Awe fills me as I notice the statues situated near the walls. Statues of people summoning different magic. My mother's hand lands on my back, guiding me to our seats. As we sit, I glance over at my mother's tense frame.

I wonder why she is so nervous.

Her gaze flits around the room. As if she's afraid of someone attacking us.

A voice draws me out of my thoughts.

"Welcome to this year's La Scelta." A man booms.

Turning my attention on him, he explains how it works.

"First, we will call your name. You will come to the center of the room. You can see that there is an altar with an ancient book. To determine your power, you must drop some blood onto the pages of the book with the dagger of fates." He holds up a short dagger with a white-silver handle. The silver is so bright that you can see your reflection in it.

"Once the book assesses your magic, the revealed element...or elements, will burst out. Showing us which element you can wield as well as an idea to the level of strength you possess."

I sit eagerly in my chair as he calls on the first person.

They confidently stride forward, gripping the dagger in their palm. Once they drip their blood, a blast of flames shoots upward. Revealing their element as fire.

I watch raptly as people are tested. Some showing two elements, some showing none. The few that possess three are taken to another room to talk about their new role in society.

"Liya Fraiser." The man calls out.

My mother freezes beside me.

She grasps my hand, leaning in close.

"Watch."

I watch as Liya slowly walks up to the book. I watch as she drips her blood. I watch as all four elements shoot upward, swirling above. I watch as she tries to run, but the guards react, shooting her with a blast of eather. I watch as she falls to the ground, dead. All because she possessed four elements.

I shake myself from the memory, thinking about how lucky I was to have shown only three elements at my ceremony. Feeling a bit off, I turn to Soren.

"I have control over earth, water, and fire," I tell him.

His eyebrows raise at the declaration. Eyeing me as we continue onward.

My legs feel a bit unsteady as we walk forward.

"Earth is easier to wield than the others. Since my magic is depleting each day, I'm mostly wielding the earth element," I explain.

Before he can respond, I feel a stab of pain in my core. The world spins around me. I stop walking, trying to ground myself. I grunt as I lose my balance, collapsing toward the ground. Strong hands catch me before I hit the hard terrain.

"What happened?" Soren demands. Slowly lowering us down.

I don't say anything, trying to blink the black spots out of my vision. He says something again, but it sounds like he's speaking through ten feet of water. The pain sharpens and spreads, making it harder to breathe. A chill seeps into my bones, my body aches in response. I focus on my ragged breathing, waiting for the pain to pass or at best, ease. After what feels like an eternity, my vision clears, and I sit up, disentangling myself from him. I wince slightly as the residual pain lingers.

"Adira? What just happened?" Soren demands.

I toss him a pained smirk. "Were you worried about me? How sweet."

He scoffs. "Worried about you? Not a chance. Try worried about breaking this oath."

I roll my eyes.

"It was my magic; I felt it in my core. The Vormr is spreading in Modereo," I reply with a wince.

"I thought it would affect me less. Being in this realm. But I still feel the impact of it spreading. The ramifications must happen to everyone from Modereo, no matter where they go." I conclude grimly.

"Well, that's not good. We'd better keep moving," Soren decides, watching as I unsteadily get to my feet.

My legs are still a bit shaky, and I sway, thinking I'm going to fall again, but steady hands hold me upright. I lift my head and inhale sharply as I realize how close our faces are.

He scowls and lets me go. *How rude.*

"Try not to faint. That would be a major inconvenience," he says through clenched teeth.

"You are such a gentleman. I'm so glad we're doing this together," I snipe back sarcastically.

He doesn't reply, just turns and starts walking deeper into the forest. Ducking under the gnarled branches that reach out over the flattened path.

Rolling my eyes, I start following him. *Even the gods must have a cruel sense of humor to give such arrogance a handsome face.*

My thoughts wander to the feel of his strong hands on me. I think about how his lips would feel on mine. His rugged good looks were a surprise after reading about everything he's accomplished. I thought he'd be a devious scoundrel. I turn slightly towards him and see one side of his mouth turn up.

"What are you smiling about?" I ask suspiciously.

"Nothing," he says with a smirk, clearly lying.

Not very convincing.

"I don't believe you."

He shrugs with a hint of amusement.

"Haven't you been wondering why I wasn't questioning you further? Or that I caught you before you collapsed to the ground?" He asks.

I tilt my head, considering his words.

"I thought the truth serum was enough proof for you." I admit, hearing the foolishness of it as I speak it aloud.

I pause at his second question. "I assume you just have fast reflexes?"

He smirks.

"That is true, but it's almost like I anticipated it." He prompts.

I play back through all our interactions.

His quick agreement to work with me. His comment when the Enid soldiers were dead. His just-in-time catch when I fell.

No, no, no, there's no way he can read my...

"Yes, princess, I can read your mind."

My eyes widen with shock, and I hit him on the chest. "WHAT THE HELL! This whole time you knew exactly what I've been thinking?"

"Ouch. And yes, I have," he states calmly with a hint of amusement.

Shooting him a glare, I squat down, pressing my hand against the hard soil. I close my eyes and call my magic to the surface. I imagine it sliding up and forming a wall in my mind.

Opening my eyes, I stand up. "Okay, let's keep moving."

"What did you do? I can't hear your thoughts. Did you put up a mental barrier?" he asks.

I smirk. "Yes. I usually have one up all the time, but with my magic depleting and there being almost no magic wielders in this realm, I thought it would be safe. How do you have that ability anyway?"

He doesn't answer right away, probably deciding whether to go with the truth or not.

"I'm not sure." He replies slowly.

I don't believe his response, but leave it be. *It's not like I'm telling him all of my secrets.*

"I see." I respond back, letting doubt seep into my tone.

He stays silent as we move between the thick trees. Staring at the ground as we walk, I get lost in the pattern of colored leaves that scatter the forest floor. A crunch echoes as I step on a brittle patch of brown leaves.

My mind shifts back to Soren's out-of-the-ordinary ability as we continue walking, wondering just how much Soren Banrs is hiding.

***

As we near the small village just outside the castle walls, I take a sharp turn to the left.

"We just have one pit stop to an ally."

"I didn't agree to this, Adira," Soren quips.

"He'll have supplies for us to sneak into the castle. Did you think we'd be able to get in successfully wearing this?" I scoff.

"If you screw me over, I'll run a sword through you before you can finish saying, 'it's not what it looks like'," Soren swears darkly.

"Well, that's reassuring." I say drily.

The gravel road narrows as we distance ourselves from the castle.

My mind drifts to the man we are about to see. I stop and turn.

"One other thing. If you hurt or betray my ally in any way, I will make your life hell." I say seriously, letting some magic flicker in my eyes to get my point across.

He smirks, unbothered.

"Consider me warned."

I don't respond, but as we start walking again, I call on my magic to put a root right where he steps. I hear him trip behind me.

"Uncalled for, witch," he sneers.

I hide my smile and ignore him. *Worth it.*

We stick to the outline of the trees until I see smoke billowing from the chimney of a small brick cottage. We look around before stepping into the clearing, but we're on the outskirts of the village, so there's not a soul in sight.

I knock twice, pause a beat, then knock two more times. The door opens to an older man with medium-length silvery hair and stormy gray eyes looking back at us.

"Adira?" he rasps out with a smile spreading across his face.

I grin. "Claude, it's so good to see you!"

We embrace, and when we pull away, he notices Soren.

He pauses, his eyes widening as he whips out his dagger. He steps in front of me protectively.

"What do you want?" Claude demands harshly.

"I don't want any trouble."

Claude huffs in disbelief.

"You may not want trouble, but trouble always seems to follow you."

Soren tilts his head at that.

"Be that as it may, I come hoping no trouble will follow."

I step forward, lowering Claude's hand.

"It's okay, Claude. He's with me." I tell him. "Temporarily."

He turns a worried expression on me.

"Do you know what you're getting yourself into?"

I shrug. "Truthfully, I don't have a lot of options right now."

I hear Soren huff behind me.

"But...he's not that bad." I grumble out.

Claude nods his head, but the distrust doesn't leave his face.

"Okay. Come on in. Both of you."

We follow him in, each of us taking a seat at the wooden table.

Glancing around, feelings of nostalgia and contentment flood me. His kitchen is stocked full of pans and jars, revealing ingredients most have never heard of. I breathe in the fresh herbs drying from the ceiling as the fireplace crackles in the back.

When everyone settles in, I lean forward on my elbows, getting right down to business.

"Okay, Claude, we don't have much time. The Vormr is spreading in Modereo; it's almost at the capital, Magia. The Stregoni are getting weaker as the land dies. I traced it back to the castle and was captured before I could get any further information. We're going back to the kingdom tonight. We'll need a carriage, clothes fit for a prince and princess from the desert kingdom of Querencia, and some expensive-looking heirlooms to flaunt at court."

"What are you going to do once you find the source? How will you stop it with your depleted magic?" Claude inquires, the concern evident in his voice.

I heave a sigh. "It's a problem. I didn't know how hard it would be to get around the castle, but I've already been caught, so they won't expect me to return. I'm hoping that finding the Astraia will answer all my questions."

Soren jumps in. "What is the Astraia?"

"It's an ancient book with information about the oldest beings in the realms. I'm hoping it will tell us where Tatsuya and Wilhema are, so we can summon them for help," I explain.

Soren opens his mouth, but I cut him off.

"And yes, it's rumored that gods and goddesses can break blood oaths. So you don't need to worry about that."

He shuts his mouth, narrowing his eyes at me. Claude eyes Soren, no doubt realizing why he's here.

I ignore him and turn back to Claude. "Can you help us?"

Claude leans back in his chair, processing everything.

"I can do that for you, dear. But you must be careful, if you aren't flawless, you will be caught. I've heard stories of others trying to sneak into the castle. All of them end the same. With death." He warns.

"We know the risk, Claude. It's something we have to do."

He lets out a resigned sigh at my response.

"Okay. Give me two hours to get everything for you. While I'm away, you both should work on the northern accent."

I nod in agreement.

He jumps up and scurries out of the room. He pauses by the door, stopping at the wooden frame and turns back.

"Also, make yourselves at home. There's a shower upstairs and towels in the closet."

I sink into my chair with relief. "Thank you for everything, Claude. You're the best."

He winks at me and disappears through the door.

I look at Soren. "You can shower first if you want. We're safe here; we can trust Claude."

I stand to leave the room.

He eyes me suspiciously. "How did you meet him?"

I turn back. "That's a story for someone *I* trust." I wink and sashay out of the room.

***

After I hear the water shut off, I grab a towel from the closet across from the bathroom. Just as I turn, the bathroom door opens, and Soren steps out with a towel around his waist. My gaze lingers on his broad chest, still glistening with water droplets, accentuating his defined muscles.

I quickly look away. My stare snagging on the dusty blue carpet. I study it intently, like it's the most interesting thing in the realm.

He clears his throat and says in a husky voice, "the bathroom is all yours."

My eyes trail back to his.

"Thanks." I whisper.

He takes a step closer to me and my breath catches as other parts of my body start to tingle. He looks down at me. We are so close our breath mingles.

He clears his throat, shattering the silence. I quickly move around him when my brain fog recedes. Latching the door shut with a soft click, I sag against it, feeling unsteady.

***

An hour later, after we'd both showered and eaten potato stew in silence, we start practicing our northern accents.

"I am certain the King will believe us." I say with an accent.

Soren seems surprised.

"How did you learn to speak it so well?" He replies, a northern lilt evident in his voice.

"My mother ensured I knew how to speak in multiple languages and accents." I supply.

"Your accent is impressive."

"With my living situation, I would always hear other accents in the castle." Soren tells me with a shrug.

"That makes sense."

We spend the next thirty minutes talking about Querencia and its customs. The accents sounding more natural with each sentence spoken.

Then, Claude bursts through the door.

"I'm back!" he announces, checking his watch. "And thirty minutes early."

"Did you get everything?" I ask hopefully.

"Well, of course I did," Claude replies with a smile.

"I have the carriage hidden about half a mile northeast. There is a man who will take you to the castle—he is very discreet. I've already paid him thirty Ellyr. He will be expecting another thirty once you leave."

Then he produces a cream-colored chest full of clothes and a box of jewelry. He hands them over to us.

"You'd better get dressed. You have a lot of work ahead of you."

We both head upstairs. Soren changes in the bathroom, and I quickly swap clothes in the bedroom.

I almost trip over the layers of silk fabric but catch myself. *No wonder women can't fight here*, I think to myself. *They can't bloody move in these dresses.* I let out a huff and exit the room.

I head back downstairs in my royal attire. Soren is already waiting with Claude. I suppress my chuckle at the frills lining his collar. Turning, my eyes latch onto stormy gray ones. Emotion floods me.

"Thank you for everything, Claude," I say thickly, heading towards his already open arms.

"You're very welcome, dear," he softly replies, his chin resting on my head.

"You look so much like your mother," he continues. "She would be so proud of you."

My chest tightens with emotion as I step back from his embrace. I try to hide the flicker of pain I feel when someone mentions my mother. On one hand, everything she forced me through has made me stronger today. On the other hand, most of it was pure torture. And when that's coming from your own mother... well, it innately messes you up.

I give him a small smile, hoping my sadness doesn't show through.

"Thank you for always being there, Claude."

"Anytime, Adira."

He pauses. "Are you certain you want to go through with this?"

"Yes. I have to."

Sighing, he gathers me in another hug. After a few moments, he reluctantly pulls back.

"You know." Claude starts quietly. "I spoke with Soren while you were finishing getting changed. He's not that bad of a guy." He admits.

I chuckle at his admission.

"No. He's not too bad." I murmur.

When I step back, Soren walks forward.

He sticks his hand out. Claude grasps it without hesitation.

"Thank you, sir. We appreciate the help."

"I'm happy to help. It's nice to see that all those terrible rumors about you aren't true," Claude says to Soren with a wink.

Soren chuckles softly at that, and we walk out the door, heading towards where our bronze carriage is hidden.

Chapter 5

As we near the hiding spot for our carriage, I stop Soren.

"Okay, time for part two of the plan," I say confidently, stepping closer to him.

He takes a step away, doubt flashing on his face.

"What is it?"

I wrinkle my nose at his blatant distrust, but... okay, fine, it's not like I trust him either.

"I'm going to alter our appearances with magic."

He looks mildly disgusted by that.

"Come on. It doesn't hurt."

A somewhat affronted look appears on his face.

"I'm not worried about it hurting." He defends, but I see the resolve in his eyes.

I smirk and grab his hand in mine, ignoring the spark I feel when our hands touch. With my other hand, I reach down to the ground and call upon my earth magic, utilizing the element to strengthen the spell.

I close my eyes and build up an image in my mind: Prince Caspian and Princess Alona from the distant kingdom of Querencia, coming to show their unwavering support for the King. Since King Dahak has only met King Harim and Queen Samara of Querencia, I thought their newly married daughter would be the safest risk.

The energy flows through my body, creating a warm embrace. It moves up my arm towards Soren. I hear his soft intake of breath and keep concentrating. I hit a wall of resistance as my image blurs in my mind. *Didn't Caspian have a scar?* I mentally sort through all the history books I've read until I reach the page about the kingdom of Querencia. A photo sits in the corner of the second page, proudly showing their respected guard. I see a jagged scar on his right forearm.

With a new image in mind, my power flows easily. I add a scar to Soren's altered appearance, then change my own. Since there are more portraits of the princess, a clear image sticks in my head.

I sway slightly as my magic strains against me, sensing my exhaustion.

I open my eyes and see my handiwork. Soren's eyes widen slightly as he looks down at his hands, the only sign of his shock.

"There." I breathe out, fatigue coating my words. "The spell should last about three days; not sure how my magic will hold after that. Our eyes are the same—they require the most amount of magic, so I thought we could risk it."

"Will King Dahak recognize your eyes?" He asks me.

"No. He never saw me. Only some guards did." I shrug off my concern.

Soren touches his face, feeling the different shape of his nose, he nods. "I was wondering how we would get into the castle in disguise. Can all Stregoni do this?"

"No. It's a rare ability, so I don't usually tell people." I reply with a pointed look.

A flash of unease crosses his face at my admission, but he nods in understanding. "Guess we'd better get going then."

As he turns, I put my hand on his arm. He stops and whirls around, a question in his eyes.

I place my hand on his cheek, patting it twice.

"Don't worry, you're still handsome." I tease as our eyes lock. My humor vanishes from his intense blue stare. I look away quickly, checking that my barrier of eather is still in place.

Without waiting for a response, I start walking ahead of him.

I hear what sounds like a huff of reluctant amusement behind me.

When we reach the carriage, we see the man Claude told us about. When he spots us, he doesn't say anything—just nods his head and climbs onto the carriage.

Okay then, I think to myself. *I guess we won't be talking to him.*

Soren and I climb into the back, and as soon as we shut the door, we are off.

***

We roll down the road in a medium-sized bronze carriage. As I watch the landscape pass by, I submit to my worries.

What if the disguise isn't good enough? What if someone finds out? I shift in my seat. Twisting my hands restlessly as I think about what may happen to us.

A warm hand encompasses mine, causing me to pause. I look at Soren questioningly. He just squeezes my hand in silent comfort, keeping his gaze straight ahead.

I gulp down unknown feelings, staring at our hands.

After a few moments, he withdraws and turns to me. "You need to be careful when showing your emotions. King Dahak is very skilled at reading people."

I school my features and look at him. "Trust me when I say I have a lot of practice with this. The question is, are you going to be able to play my loving, caring husband?" I raise an eyebrow.

He turns away, and when he looks back, the heat of his gaze makes me feel like I am the only thing in the world, and everything else has disappeared. Much to my dismay, I feel heat creep into my cheeks.

I clear my throat. "You'll be fine."

He smirks and turns to stare out the window. I look out mine as well and see that we are approaching the front gates of the castle.

The carriage slows as we near a row of guards. Our mysterious driver conveys who we are. The guards' peek through the window and wave us through. I push down the nerves during the short ride to the castle steps.

Too soon, the carriage stops. I feign confidence as I step out with renewed determination. I cannot fail. I will not fail.

I look to Soren and hold out my hand; he takes it without hesitation. We step towards the castle and tell the Lord Steward our names, so he can announce us to the court. As we wait, I notice that a heavy pressure has settled over me. I probe our appearances and find they are still strongly in place. I shake off the feeling as we are urged through the doors. My pendant burns slightly, the pain becoming sharper as we stride down the hall. My hands itch to take it off, but my mother's voice stops me from doing that. *You must never take this necklace off. No matter what. You will know when the time is right.* More secrets that she never elaborated on.

We had sent a letter in advance to the King from Querencia, stating our arrival and purpose. I altered the situation with magic to make the letter appear as though it had arrived two weeks prior.

We step through the large doors and into the spacious corridor. I try not to be distracted by the sights around me. Long silk fabric drapes from the tall stained-glass windows, expressing beautiful depictions of different beings. My brow furrows at some of the images. *Odd, I don't recognize some of those creatures.* The corridor stretches endlessly before me with marble statues and elegant tapestries lining the walls. The sound of footsteps echoes off the impossibly high ceilings. I watch the guard's movement. Most seem to stride down this hall quickly, stopping by select drapery. I make note of those specific renderings; certain they lead to the dark tunnels below. I turn my focus forward, surprised we have already reached the end. The doors swing open for us, revealing a regal dining hall.

The heavy pressure I felt before suddenly makes sense. My eyes find the wall to the right, I hide my shudder as my magic flares out. I grasp at my power, reigning it in before it can show. I struggle to keep my breathing even at the close call.

The weight of the wards against my magic fades to a dull ache as horror replaces it.

The last Teràstios head is brutally spiked to the wall.

My stomach turns as I think of those magnificent creatures hunted by the monster sitting in front of me.

My thoughts drift back to a younger time when the Teràstios flew free. Nights were filled with stories of their quests. The only time there was a semblance of normalcy in my childhood. We used to worship them for their godlike attributes. I think of their broad wings and long horns that I will never get to see because they were all murdered shortly before I was born.

Because of King Dahak.

I swallow my bile and look the monster in the eyes. I give a smile and bow. "Thank you for welcoming us into your kingdom, Your

Majesty. We are most excited to meet the man behind the impressive legends."

His dark blue eyes are almost black, threatening to pull you into their depths. I hide the shiver that travels up my spine. The pain from my pendant thrums into a low ache, settling into my chest. But the burning doesn't increase, it stays steady. *Strange.* I think, eyeing the man in front of me.

He smiles his fake smile at all the guests around the table. "Well, I always welcome my fellow rulers and their families. Please, have a seat."

"Thank you, Your Majesty," Soren says with a bow of his head.

Soren pulls out my chair, and I lower myself into it with the elegance of a court-trained princess. He sinks into the chair next to me.

"The journey went well, I presume?" the King asks, turning our attention back to him.

While Soren speaks, I study the King's sharp face. If I didn't know how foul he was, I might be swayed by his charm. He uses his short blond hair and piercing stare to his advantage.

"The two weeks just flew by, Your Majesty. We found ourselves looking forward to arriving to your alluring lands," Soren says earnestly.

King Dahak brushes away the comment. "And how are your lands? I'm afraid I've never had the opportunity to visit King Harim and Queen Samara in their kingdom...or meet their daughter."

He pauses, tilting his head in mock consideration.

"Curious. I make it a point to remember all royal lineages." He gives us a shrewd look.

My blood freezes. I plaster on a warm smile and speak before Soren can.

"Oh, it is simply gorgeous at home—sand dunes for miles, Your Majesty. You will have to make a trip to visit our kingdom sometime in the future, when you aren't too busy with your own, of course." I inject innocence into my voice, hoping my revulsion doesn't show.

"As for my existence," I force out a small laugh, "my parents would often get lost in the politics of running a kingdom and forget I was around. I spent many afternoons in the quiet library by myself. As I'm sure you know, one can get very busy with the lives of many people under their rule." I finish with a shy smile. *Please believe it.* I think with conviction.

"Well, I do know how it can be, Alona. Hopefully, you were still able to learn a lot from them. I will have to come and see your kingdom with my own eyes as soon as I am able," the King says, suspicion lingering behind his eyes and words. I bite my lip, fighting the urge to release my power onto him.

He turns to Soren. "Caspian, are you looking forward to being King?"

I feel eyes on me from the left. Subtly shifting in my seat, I glance at the culprit. We lock eyes. Their gaze narrows slightly before turning their attention back to their plate. Further down the table, I notice two ladies whispering to each other while peeking toward Soren and I.

My grip tightens on my cutlery as I fight to shift in my seat. A bead of sweat rolls down my back from the stares.

Do they know? I question to myself. I keep imagining them jumping to their feet, yelling 'imposters, imposters.'

Soren laughs jovially. "I am in no rush, Your Majesty. Still learning the ropes from King Harim and Queen Samara. They have a lot to teach me."

"Hmm, I see, I see," the King murmurs.

I subtly scan the table, taking in all the nobles. Most carry an air of caution as they converse, like they are worried that saying the wrong thing will result in the King's temper. One woman at the end of the table keeps sneaking glances at one of the guards, I notice his cheeks darken slightly at the attention.

"So. You must oversee the trades that come to us. What did you think about the last shipment?" King Dahak inquires with a wicked smile.

My heart skips a beat at his question. *We don't know this.*

Soren seems unfazed.

"Honestly, Your Majesty, the last shipment was not one of our best. We are searching for a new cave of sandstones. I understand how useful they are to you and your kingdom. On behalf of Querencia, I do apologize for our oversight but can guarantee the next shipment will be more to your liking."

The King relaxes his shrewd look when Soren answers.

"Yes. See that it is." He responds, waving a dismissive hand.

I fight to keep my expression neutral. *How did he know that?*

King Dahak seems to lose interest and returns to his meal, polishing it off in record time.

Once he's done, he lounges back in his chair, letting his eyes wander leisurely over everyone at the table. Everyone tries to finish as fast as they can without seeming improper. My stomach twists as his gaze flits past me, then bounces back. I pretend not to notice, focusing my attention on a piece of broccoli. I daintily impale it with my fork, bringing it up to my mouth. As I chew, I smile thinly at the person beside me, he returns the gesture with a tight smile. Finally, I feel his gaze move on. I almost slump in relief.

He abruptly stands. We all rise with him.

"I will see you all tomorrow evening for the ball." His tone implies that it is required.

As soon as he leaves, everyone starts dispersing to their respective rooms. Soren holds out his arm for me to take, I grip it and try to ignore the stares.

Two guards approach us and offer to escort us to our room. We thank them and follow them down the hall. I discreetly glance around as we walk, trying to absorb as many details about the castle's layout as possible.

As we turn the corner of a particularly long hall, I see the guard with short black hair and dark skin move swiftly around another corner, his hand resting on the back of one of the ladies from dinner. I file that information away for later.

After many twists and turns, we finally reach our room and thank the guards. Once inside, I close the door and look at Soren, widening my eyes to signal him to stay silent.

I head over to my trunk and pull out the small potted flower I packed to recharge my magic. Plunging my hands into the soil, I call upon my earth magic to scan the room for any listening charms. Pressure shoves back at me as my magic flows through the space. I grit my teeth from the strength of the wards, pushing more magic out. Soren watches me silently. Once I'm certain the room isn't compromised, I turn to him.

"We aren't being listened to or watched at the moment," I exclaim.

"Thanks for checking, and good job at dinner. It was obvious the King was interrogating us," Soren says, then a frown shadows his face.

"What is it?" I ask, put off by his expression.

"I don't know." He closes his eyes, and I watch his face scrunch up.

"King...mind...block." He whispers the words to himself then seems confused, as if he can't remember what he just said.

"Can you read the King's mind?" I ask.

His features clear from my words. "No."

He shakes his head in disbelief.

"I've never been able to read his mind. Why couldn't I remember that?"

"He's more powerful than he lets on. He must be getting power from somewhere. I've heard of dark magic that can be used to confuse those who touch it."

Soren appears lost in thought at that.

"There's no way he'd be able to control all these kingdoms without something to hold over them." I remark.

"There's been rumors about Dahak using dark magic. Usually, it's from the people who I have been sent to execute."

"That would make sense. He would want to squash those rumors before they spread. Especially since he is such an advocate for non-magic folk."

Soren nods as if that adds up.

I think about King Dahak controlling the Umbrai. And how he can block mental attacks. Something isn't right. Fatigue latches onto me, so I decide to deliberate over him tomorrow.

"Thank goddess that's over," I say, letting out a breath of relief and plopping onto the bed. I let all the tense thoughts of dinner out of my mind.

I feel a low pulsing of power from somewhere in the castle. I wince as my mind focuses on the power constantly being drained from me, surrendering to the pressure from the wards. I can feel my magic screaming at me to get away from this place.

"There is something here. I can feel it," I tell Soren.

"What do you feel?" he asks.

"A low thrum of magic. My own power recognizes it as a threat. I just want to find the Astraia and get out of here."

"How did you learn about this book?" Soren asks, his lips turned down.

"An old philosopher in my realm told me that locating Tatsuya and Wilhema would stop the Vormr. My best chance is to find them and wake them. I know the Astraia is kept here by the King."

"He keeps most of his older books in the library that's in the east wing. Lucky for us, the ballroom is also in the east, so that should make it easier."

"Okay, great. Can't wait," I reply tiredly, ending the conversation with a tone of finality.

That's when I look around the room and realize there's only one bed. Soren realizes the same thing the moment I do. He grips the back of his neck but doesn't say anything. I shrug like it doesn't matter.

Okay, not a problem. I repeat to myself, even as a flood of warmth fills my body at the thought of sharing a bed with him.

I rise from the bed to wash up in the bathroom. As I pass him, he mutters something indecipherable under his breath.

In the bathroom, I look at myself in the mirror and give myself a little pep talk.

It's not a big deal, Adira. The bed is so big you won't even touch. Do not think about his chiseled chest again. I pause and double-check my mental barriers. Once I'm certain they are secure, I take a deep breath and head back out into the bedroom.

Soren heads into the bathroom as I crawl into the large bed. A moment later, he finishes and enters the main room. The bed dips as he climbs in.

Suddenly, the bed doesn't seem so big anymore.

Soren turns to me, staring for a moment before speaking.

"You have..." A flash of vulnerability crosses his face, he quickly schools his features. "...such strange eyes."

I huff out a laugh at that comment.

"Thanks," I say sarcastically. *Like I haven't heard that before.* My green eyes with a thin ring of violet in them always draw attention.

"They," He pauses, grunting slightly as if it pains him to say, "are nice."

I turn my head in shock.

"Thanks," I repeat in a whisper. I then notice that I've subconsciously moved closer to his warmth.

This brings our faces much closer, and we both pause. I feel my body flush with anticipation. *Anticipation?* If only my brain could control my body. *This is my enemy, for goddess sake.* We stare at each other a beat longer, then both turn onto our backs, shifting back to our prospective sides.

"Goodnight."

"Night," he grunts.

Slowly, we both drift off to sleep.

***

When I wake, I feel a heavy arm across my stomach. I slowly turn my head and see Soren pressed against me. My body becomes aware of all the places we're touching.

How the hell did this happen? This is the biggest bed I've ever been in.

I try to move my body away as slow as I can before he wakes up. My leg brushes against something hard. I freeze, eyes widening. I hear him shuffle, and glance over at him.

"Adira," Soren sleepily says as he opens his eyes.

He freezes when he realizes that he's clinging to me. He stays still for a moment, keeping me trapped in his embrace. My heart starts beating faster. Then he leaps up off the bed. He shakes his head in confusion then levels me with a glare like it was my fault. Before I can call him out, he moves swiftly across the room.

He runs his hands through his short brown hair, looking more disheveled than I've ever seen him look.

"I'm going to take a shower," he mumbles and turns to the bathroom.

The door quickly slams shut, and a minute later, the water turns on. I go to shake off any strangeness from waking up in his arms and find that it didn't feel strange; it felt right.

It must be my magic. The constant heaviness of it is making me feel unbalanced. I reason with myself. *Yep. Just my magic.*

Chapter 6

Later that morning, as we walk out of our room, we're joined by the two guards assigned to us. They take us down to the dining hall for breakfast. Fortunately, the King isn't present; unfortunately, the rest of the court is.

Hopefully, everyone will be too busy to pay us any attention.

I glance at the Terástios head on the wall, and my stomach flips. I say a silent prayer to it as I take my seat.

"So," the lively lady from the previous night says as soon as we sit down, "how did you two meet?" She looks between us, awaiting an answer.

"Oh, my name is Emma, by the way," she adds, "and this is my husband, Rados." She gestures to the man beside her.

I smile politely, recognizing her as the one who was sneaking away with the guard.

"Nice to meet you both. Well, my parents were trying to find suitable bachelors for me from different kingdoms. But Caspian had been our youngest Captain of the Guard ever, so we both grew up in the castle while he was training and fell in love over the years."

I turn and smile lovingly at Soren, only to find he is already looking at me with affection in his eyes.

I internally shake my head at the rush of feelings from his gaze. *He's acting, Adira. He despises you. And more importantly, you despise him.*

All the ladies at the table sigh at the display of affection. We turn to them and smile.

"Anyone can see how in love you two are," Emma says adoringly.

What did this woman just say? We must be great actors.

We make idle chit-chat for the rest of breakfast and then excuse ourselves to explore the grounds.

"Oh! I would love to show you around the grounds," Emma says, jumping up. My earlier hope fades at the offer.

Soren and I exchange a quick glance but realize we can't get out of it without seeming suspicious.

Emma sends her husband a look, and Rados grunts out, "Caspian, why don't you join us men?"

"I appreciate the offer, Rados. I would be honored," Soren replies.

He turns back to me to press a kiss to my cheek. "Be careful," he whispers.

I wave as they head off, and Emma loops her arm around mine.

"Well, aren't you two just the cutest?" she says, dragging me toward the garden. I smile at her and change the subject.

"These gardens are beautiful," I say. "How long have you been in the court?"

"All my life," Emma says proudly. "My mother was one of the King's mistresses, so I know every nook and cranny of the castle."

I glance at her out of the corner of my eye. "That must come in handy when you're sneaking around with your guard," I say boldly.

She freezes. "Why would you say that? That's not true. I love my husband very much."

"Don't worry, Emma. It's not that obvious. I'm very good at reading people." I pause, thinking about her subtle glances at dinner the other night. "Plus, I saw you two sneaking around last night."

She senses my sincerity and releases a breath. "Thank gods. I've been dying to talk about this with someone for years! There are secret passageways behind some of the tapestries that lead to rooms underground. We sneak there at night to meet."

I hide my involuntary shiver at the thought of those secret passageways I was running through just days ago. They span the entire underground of the castle and contain the prison cells, which I'm unfortunately familiar with. The only reason I escaped was because one of the guards was ignorant enough to drink too much on the job, and I was able to grab his key. Luckily, a sliver of my magic slipped through my drug-oppressed system, and I used it to guide me to the forest.

I keep her talking about her secret romance with Talil, her guard. Eventually, the afternoon arrives, and we part ways to get ready for the ball tonight.

I get back to the room before Soren, so I change into the dress Claude got me. Even I must admit it's gorgeous. It's a floor-length deep green silk dress with long sleeves and gold accents. I finish putting my hair up with the gold feather clasp just as Soren walks through the door.

I turn to him and see him pause as he looks me up and down. Heat fills his gaze.

"I guess you don't look terrible," Soren says huskily.

I twirl a bit to hide the redness of my cheeks from his stare. "Not the best, but not the worst compliment I've gotten. Claude did an amazing job finding this."

We hold each other's gaze as time stretches around us.

"Well, I better get changed too," Soren says, shaking his head as he turns toward the bathroom.

As soon as he closes the door, it feels like a balloon of tension leaks out of the room. I take a deep breath and think, *What the hell was that?*

***

As we step into the ballroom, we see everyone from the court dressed in their finest attire. I must admit, the room looks impressive, from the high vaulted ceiling to the intricate detail of the red and gold marble tiles. I glance to my right and spot a table stocked full of all kinds of food.

We take two steps in, and a waiter appears with a tray of champagne flutes. We each take one and nod our thanks.

Whispers reach my ears as we stride deeper into the room. Curious and assessing. Fortunately, King Dahak seems distracted by the several ladies sitting around him.

We linger near the food table while Soren talks to a duke about foreign affairs. I look around the room and lock eyes with the King. I nod politely and give a small curtsy. He nods back and holds my stare, long enough to make me uneasy. The band changes to a song with a quick tempo, my heart follows the rhythm. I keep a shy expression on my face and turn my thoughts to Soren's heated gaze from earlier. Latching onto that feeling, I summon a blush. Trying to convey that I'm pleased by the King's attention. Finally, he returns his gaze back to his mistresses.

Someone taps me on the shoulder, and I turn. It's Soren, his arm stretched out. I give a small smile, silently communicating with my eyes, *what are you doing?*

Through his smile, he says, "They encouraged me to ask you to dance."

I elegantly take his hand, and he twirls me toward him in one swift motion.

I gasp as my hand lands on his chest to steady myself. He smirks, his hand drifting to my lower back, spinning me onto the dance floor.

The music shifts to an intimate, upbeat waltz.

The feeling of everyone's eyes on us causes my nerves to rise. *If everyone is watching, we might as well give them a convincing show.*

I match his every step. Our eyes lock, and I find that I can't look away. Heat flares in all the spots where our bodies connect. My face flushes as we glide across the dance floor, oblivious to the other dancers. Yet somehow, we move so perfectly together that we never bump into another couple.

A low strum from the cello signals a change, and he dips me with the melody. The beat shifts to a wistful tone, momentarily creating a more somber atmosphere. My stomach swooshes as he slowly whisks me back up toward him. Our foreheads touch, and we look into each other's eyes. We sway, lost in each other's gaze, as the song draws to an end.

As the guests begin to applaud, we move to the side of the dance floor. The tempo changes back to a jubilant tone. The weight of the noble's stares disappear as they head to the dance floor. I breathe out the worry I didn't know I was feeling.

Soren leans down to my ear.

"Guess I can actually call you a princess now," he whispers with a smirk.

"Still not a princess," I murmur back.

"You look like a princess," his voice gentle, almost caressing. Heat rises to my cheeks at the uncharacteristic softness in his voice.

We hold each other's gaze until the band starts another song, shattering the moment.

My fleeting haze clears, and I whisper, "I'm going to slip away to look around. Cover for me if someone notices I'm gone."

As I turn to go, he stops me with a light touch. Then, he pulls me close, gripping my arms tightly as he discreetly glances around the ballroom.

"Be careful, Adira. King Dahak doubles his guards during balls."

I give him a shallow nod as I move out of his warm embrace. Turning, I stroll unhurriedly through the crowd, nodding and exchanging polite greetings as I pass. I make my way toward the bathroom, then slip further down the corridor. My heart pulses steadily, matching the low throbbing of my pendant. I grasp it in my hand, wondering why it's reacting to the magic in this place.

Thankfully, Soren gave me a detailed layout of the castle, so I have some idea of where to go. I take two left turns and reach two large wooden doors on my right. Slipping into the room, I reach into my hidden pocket to retrieve the earth amulet I made earlier. An earth amulet is a token crafted from natural materials, providing a reserve of magic—handy since my powers seem to deplete so quickly here.

Closing my eyes, I stretch my magic out to sense any presence in the room. Once I'm certain it's clear, I reach out again, searching for the book I need.

I feel a tug toward the right side of the room and head that way. I follow the sensation to a dusty section of shelves. The books are covered in a layer of thick dust. They all appear old, but only one stands out as ancient. I grab it, its worn leather feels like it might disintegrate in my hands.

I open it, coughing as dust rises. Skimming through the pages, I pause on an entry about Tatsuya and Wilhema. Before I can read it, the sound of whispered voices interrupts. I freeze in place, straining to listen. Someone giggles and I hear the unmistakable sound of sloppy kisses. *Great. I might get caught by a secret tryst.* Their footsteps echo on the tiled floor as they start moving. *Please don't pick this room. Any room but this one.* I plead. The sound dims as they move further down the corridor.

Breathing a sigh of relief, I quickly turn my attention back to the book. Reading it as fast as I can before another couple decides to use this room.

Just as I place it back on the shelf, I hear footsteps.

My heart races. I stiffen as they grow louder. I curse under my breath and hide deeper within the stacks of books.

The door creaks open, and the sound of boots echoes on the tiled floor. Peeking through the shelves, I see a guard methodically checking each row.

I mentally groan. *Since when do they do their jobs so thoroughly?*

Crouching at the edge of the shelf, I prepare to surprise him. Just before my shelf, he pauses. Holding my breath, I stay silent. A clock ticks threateningly in the background.

As he rounds the corner to my shelf, I see his eyes widen in shock, his mouth opening to speak.

I quickly press my finger to his temple, releasing a burst of magic. He slumps to the ground unconscious.

Grunting under his weight, I prop him against the shelves, making it look as if he took a seat on purpose. Then, I grab a forgotten glass of whiskey that was sitting on a nearby table. I pour it over his clothes. The air fills with the sharp scent of liquor.

Turning away, I scold myself. *He saw you, Adira. Focus.*

I close my eyes, planting an image in his mind of himself drinking instead of encountering me.

I turn to go, but a thread pulls at me. Looking left, I notice an object sitting on its own shelf. I step closer, sensing memory magic. Deciding I can't risk it, I leave the magic stamp alone, walking back to the door.

Slowly, I ease the door open, wincing as the hinges creak. Glancing down the hallway, I slip out and softly close the door behind me.

I make it back to the party without incident, scanning the room for Soren. I spot him talking to Emma near one of the gold pillars and head toward them.

Emma notices me first, her expression concerned as she meets me halfway.

"Are you feeling all right? Caspian said you were feeling under the weather."

I glance at Soren over her shoulder.

"Yes, I was. I'm feeling much better now, thanks, Emma."

Soren steps in.

"But I think it's best if we retire for the night. Let's go, Adira."

I tense. Soren's grip tightens at his mistake. Emma has a puzzled look.

"Adira? Who's Adira?" Emma asks, her nose wrinkled in confusion.

A beat of silence passes.

"It's, um, my middle name. Sometimes he likes to call me that." I explain to her.

"That's odd." She remarks tentatively.

Soren jumps in, playing to Emma's romantic side.

"Her middle name means powerful and strong. How could I not call her that?" He says, pushing adoration into his voice as he pulls me tight to his side. I place my hand on his chest, sending him a soft smile.

Her expression clears.

"That is so sweet." She says, dabbing at the corner of her eyes. "You are such a wonderful couple."

I smile thinly.

"Thank you, Emma."

"I apologize if it caused you any confusion." Soren tells her, shooting her a charming smile.

She waves it off.

"No problem at all. Have a good evening you two."

"You as well." I respond warmly.

Soren takes my elbow, steering me toward the exit.

We nod politely, bidding goodnight to the other guests. Luckily, others are leaving as well, making our early departure seem less suspicious. My vision blurs slightly as we walk down the long hall. The loss of my magic and adrenaline weakening me. I lean into Soren, using his arm to relieve some of the weight. He squeezes my hand, pulling me closer.

Once we're back in our room, I head to the nightstand and grab my plant with shaking hands. I dig my hands into the soil, feeling the immediate flow of magic replenishing within me. This realm feels like there's a blanket smothering my powers, making them harder to access.

I stretch my magic around the room, checking for any listening charms. Finding none, I turn to Soren.

"I know what we need to do next," I announce.

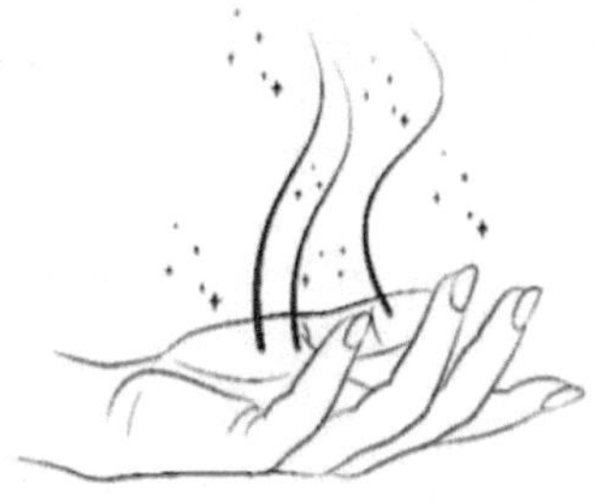

Chapter 7

After I explain my plan to Soren and recount my run-in with the guard, we both pass out from the day's festivities. None of the tension from yesterday lingers.

When I wake, I find myself staring at Soren's face.

Bolting upright, I rush to the mirror.

"Shit," I swear.

When I turn back around, Soren is awake, his brows furrowed in concern.

"Your face," he says, pointing. "I thought you said three days."

"Yeah, well, my powers are getting weaker the longer the Vormr spreads."

He runs a hand through his hair in frustration.

"If your magic keeps fading this fast, we're going to run out of options."

Guilt and anxiety roll around in my gut.

"I know." I say flatly.

"How are we going to get out of the castle?"

I focus inward, trying to gauge how much magic I have left. I press my hands into the soil, feeling the faint, dwindling pulse of energy.

"I could alter your face one more time—for about an hour."

"What about you, Adira?"

I glance around the room and spot a sheer black veil. Draping it over my face, I reply, "We can use magic to send word of my cousin's death. That will explain my mourning and justify a hasty exit."

A sharp knock on the door startles us both. "We are here to escort you to the dining hall, Your Royal Highnesses," a voice announces from the other side.

We exchange tense glances. "It'll have to do," I whisper to Soren.

He nods and gathers our belongings swiftly. While he works, I press my hands into the soil once more, drawing on the last dregs of my magic to alter Soren's face again.

I extend my magic further, picturing the King's messenger in my mind. Focusing hard, I push the image of a letter arriving with news of our cousin's passing. The crest of Querencia fights back, the symbol making it hard to copy. I create one with a missing star, my power flows easier since it is not the true emblem. Uncertainty trickles in at the error, and I pray it's small enough that it goes unnoticed.

I feel it draining from the bottom of my reserves, but I keep pushing. If we don't make it out of here, what's the point of holding on to any magic at all?

When the illusion is complete and the messenger is on his way to the King with the missive, my body sways.

As soon as I open my eyes, darkness creeps in at the edges of my vision. The last thing I see is Soren rushing across the room to catch me.

***

The sound of rapid footsteps rouses me. Blinking away the disorientation, I fight the urge to slip back into darkness.

When I fully open my eyes, I see that I'm lying on the bed, and Soren is pacing at the foot of it. As I start to push myself up, he snaps his head towards me.

"Are you okay?" he asks sharply.

"I'm fine. I just used more magic than I should have." I admit with a grimace.

I glance around, panic rising in my chest.

"How long was I out? We need to get moving, or else the spell will wear off."

"Don't worry. You were only out for a moment. I told the guards you were still getting ready. They left and came back almost immediately with the news of your 'cousin's' passing. They're giving us a moment to grieve. The bags are packed—once you're well enough, we'll go."

I exhale a breath of relief.

"Thank the goddess. I'm good to go."

I swing my legs over the side of the bed and push myself up. The room tilts, and my vision swims, forcing me to grip the wooden frame for balance.

Soren's frustrated voice cuts through the fog.

"Are you sure you're okay to move?"

I bristle at his tone.

"I'm going to have to be." I snap, meeting his gaze pointedly. "Jerk." I mumble under my breath.

He nods once, ignoring the insult.

"Good. You can use my arm for support—it'll look like I'm comforting you."

I drape the black veil over my face and take his arm.

As we cross the room, I shake off the cloud lingering in my mind. I've been in worse situations; surely, I can make it out of this castle without passing out.

The guards escort us to the castle's entrance, and we reach the carriage without incident. The King's right hand appears, informing us that King Dahak is tied up with matters of state but sends his deepest condolences for our 'loss'. We thank him politely and step into the carriage.

Once we're out of sight, I slump into my seat, the last of my energy drained from me.

As consciousness slips away, my final thought is bitterly ironic: I've now fainted in front of an enemy twice.

***

When I wake up, I feel a thousand times better. I open my eyes and look around, spotting Soren by a river. The illusion over him gone.

I start to stand and notice I'm covered in dirt. I laugh quietly to myself and glance over at him.

"You didn't have to cover me with dirt, you know," I say, trying to hide my smile.

The corner of his mouth twitches upwards.

"Well, I noticed you always touch the soil for more magic, so I thought I'd give it a try."

He looks me up and down, a touch of concern in his gaze.

"Are you feeling better now?" He asks in a soft tone.

I relax under his stare. The tension from the situation melting away.

"Much," I reply, looking around. "Where are we?"

"About thirty minutes from Claude's. I thought you'd want to be awake when you saw him again. I paid the man driving the carriage thirty Ellyr, and he walked away wordlessly, disappearing deeper into the forest. He was strange."

"He was definitely odd," I huff out with a chuckle.

"Okay," I continue, "let's go then."

Excitement over seeing Claude again trumps my exhaustion.

Soren walks over to me, holding out his hand. I grab it. He pulls me up, his hand settling on my waist briefly before letting go. My mind travels back to our dance yesterday and the intimate feeling of being in his arms. I shake my head, casting the thought away. *Focus, Adira. I tell myself. You don't have time for distractions. But...what an attractive distraction it would be.*

I check my mental barrier. Horror grasping me when I find them down. Summoning my magic, I quickly snap them up.

Hopefully, I wasn't projecting. Embarrassment trickles in from my previous thoughts.

We start heading back towards Claude's to grab our belongings. I notice Soren eyeing me as we walk.

I stop in my tracks.

"What do you keep looking at?" I demand.

"Just making sure you don't pass out again, princess." He says, pressing two fingers to my neck.

"Are you checking my pulse?" I ask dumbly. Shock blocking my senses.

"Yes."

A burst of delight erupts in my chest at his concern. I ignore the intense feeling.

"Aww, are you worried about me, Soren?" I tease.

"Worried? Try inconvenienced at having to carry you," he says with a slight tilt of his head.

I peer at him with a smirk.

"Whatever you say."

He scoffs, then falls quiet for a moment.

"You had a strange reaction when we entered the King's dining hall the other day. Did something happen?" he asks curiously.

I inhale sharply, thinking of the King's treacherous wall décor.

"The Terástios head on the wall—do you know the history?"

He shrugs.

"Only a little bit."

"Well, in our realm, they are revered, majestic creatures. King Dahak hunted them for sport in your realm. In ours, we worshipped them. They were godlike beings, and some people were rumored to be able to bond with them, creating a formidable team. I've only ever dreamed of meeting one, but they were all killed shortly before I was born—because of King Dahak."

I feel a surge of anger as the King's smug face creeps into my mind.

"That's terrible. I had no idea they were like that. My father told me we had to destroy them, or they'd ruin villages and slaughter humans." He pauses, seeming lost in thought.

"When I was very young, we'd have school drills about them. We'd have to swiftly and silently move to the basement of the school. The teachers would make it believable. Window's shattered, the ground would rumble, and a screeching noise would pierce the air. It definitely instilled fear into us."

My mind views the scene as vividly as a magic stamp would show. I think about young kids having to experience that terror and my heart aches with sadness.

He shakes his head. "I wonder what else was just a lie put forward by the King."

"Anything with power would be a threat to him. That's why he builds fear into society. It's the only way he's managed to control the kingdom—through fear."

I see Soren nodding, lost in thought.

I let my own mind drift for the remainder of the short journey to Claude's, thinking about how King Dahak may have gained control through fear, but now he maintains it with some kind of unknown power.

***

I see the smoke billowing from Claude's cottage before it even comes into view. Silence fills the forest. I tilt my head, listening closer, but not even a bird chirps. Alarm takes root in my gut. Before we step into the clearing, I stretch my magic out to check for any unwanted visitors.

Sensing nothing, we head over to the door. I shiver at the unnatural stillness in the air.

We amble up the steps and knock.

After a minute, I start to get worried. Soren voices my concerns.

"He wouldn't just leave without a sign. Something's wrong."

I stretch my magic inside the cabin, but I'm blocked by a ward.

"Damn it, of course he'd have wards up," I mutter.

Soren grumbles something about a paranoid old man, and we both head around to one of the windows to look in.

As we walk back down the steps, my eyes scan the area, and I notice his garden is trampled. Dread latches onto me. *He would never let that happen.* I think grimly as we walk along the side of the house.

When we glance through the window, my stomach drops. The place is a wreck. Pots litter the floor. A chair is lying on its side. A broken table leg rests on the ground, the jagged end tainted with dry blood. I immediately pull on my magic to analyze the scene.

A knock echoes at the door—Claude goes to answer it. Guards march past him and start ransacking the house. One grabs Claude by the tunic, shouting in his face about hiding the witch. Claude argues he isn't hiding anyone. They seize his head, slamming it onto the table, yelling for the location of the traitor. The table breaks from the force. He scrambles for a piece. He grips the broken table leg, thrusting it forward. It goes into one of the guards' legs. He shouts in pain. The other guard forces him back onto the ground, pressing him for more information. He refuses to say anything.

They drag him towards the door. He thrashes, trying to break free, knocking things over along the way. Claude manages to kick out a leg, almost taking one of the guards down. The guard holding him swears, nodding to another. The second guard nods back and strikes Claude on the head, knocking him out cold. They haul him outside, loading him into the back of a carriage.

I blink out of the memory to find Soren shaking me.

"Adira!"

I jerk away, but his tight grip keeps me in place.

"What are you doing?!"

"You went into some kind of trance and wouldn't respond," he says, a hint of concern in his voice.

"I was watching a magic stamp of what happened," I explain.

He looks at me blankly, still holding onto my arms.

"A memory," I elaborate.

He blinks once.

"A what?"

"It's when Stregoni use an echo of magic to reveal a scene from the past. Some are strong enough to pull you into the memory, while most just let you observe."

He still doesn't let go. His gaze wanders over my body, as if he has to physically ensure I'm alright with his own eyes.

My cheeks darken from his attention.

Once he seems appeased, he releases his hold.

Shaking his head to himself, he scowls, shattering the moment.

"Well, tell me before you do that. I thought your magic had possessed you or something—and I still need help getting out of this blood oath."

I roll my eyes at his response, quickly sobering up as I think about what I saw. Panic building up in me as the scene plays through my mind again.

Soren breaks my thoughts.

"So, what happened?"

"The guards came for him. They must have known we were here." I tell him, tone laden with guilt.

"I don't know where they took him. But he didn't say anything about us."

"There are several prisons he could have been taken to. Or he could have been sent straight to the kingdom." Soren says with a wince.

I exhale deeply, trying not to let my thoughts wander to the fate that's befallen Claude. Because of us.

"Come on. We need to get in and grab our stuff before the guards come back to scout the area."

We head around the back and let ourselves in. Upstairs, we move the trunk at the foot of the bed to the side. Lifting a floorboard, we retrieve our packs.

Good thing Claude told us to hide our things, I think bitterly.

We quickly slip back into the cover of the forest.

Once I scan the area again, we turn to face each other.

I hesitate before speaking.

Should we try to save Claude first? I ask myself. My magic pulses weakly in response. *But we can't just leave him. He was imprisoned because of us.* I try to reason with my magic.

Unsurprisingly, it doesn't answer me. Leaving me to my own deliberations. I sigh in defeat, knowing what I must choose.

"We don't have time to look for Claude right now."

Soren looks at me, surprised.

"That's what I was going to say—I just didn't think you'd agree."

I grimace.

"I wish we could drop everything, but I can feel my magic depleting. We need to go to the goddesses. Once we're there, we can ask about Claude as well."

"And where are we supposed to find these all-knowing goddesses? Why would we even trust what's in the Astraia?" Soren asks skeptically.

"Because I skimmed through the book first, and some of the information matched the history books in Modereo."

"And we can trust the history books in Modereo?" He questions.

I hesitate. "I think so. We don't have many options at this point."

He pauses, as if weighing the plan in his head.

"Hopefully, they are accurate."

I nod in agreement.

"What do you know about the Arae?" I ask Soren.

"Not much. There was very little about them in our history books," he admits.

I take a deep breath and jump into the story that was told to us as young kids. "*Long ago, before life existed, the Arae found this world. They decided it needed life, so they created six beings. The goddesses; Fadama Desai, Tatsuya Desai and Wilhema Daray, and gods; Tiamat Daray, Conri Aamon, and Cain Aamon were created. Eventually, the Arae became uninterested in these beings and decided to create new, different life. Thus, came the humans. Once humans started to show fear, some of the gods and goddesses came to crave the power associated with this emotion. These higher beings made themselves known and ruled over the humans. Tatsuya and Wilhema instilled magic into some of the bloodlines so humans could evolve with magic and protect themselves if need be. They created a space between worlds for higher beings to rest and exist, they called it Noelani. They left humankind to go live in Noelani. The humans fared on their own and put in place their own systems. Naturally, the Stregoni and non-magic folk separated to different areas of the world. King Dahak came into power and started killing the Teràstios. Before he could finish killing them all, the Arae sensed an imbalance in the world and split it in two. Creating two realms that were difficult to pass between. The Arae renamed the realms, Modereo, which is where most magic wielders reside, and Enelon, where the humans with no powers resided.*

I glance at Soren, "I found proof in that book of where the entrance to Noelani is. It's in the Erontil mountains. We need to go there to wake the goddesses."

Soren processes this. "Why did the Arae care about the Teràstios? Seems like something they wouldn't bother with."

"I think they cared more about the power shift. The Teràstios were powerful creatures. Killing that many caused a vast change in energy. The Arae would've felt that shift and investigated. They must've not liked the blatant disregard for higher power and retaliated."

"That seems plausible." Soren conveys.

"Who knows what the Arae think. They are the oldest beings in this world. I can't even fathom being alive that long." I shiver at the thought.

"True. I can't even begin to imagine what that would feel like."

"Although, if you live that long, you get to experience the different shifts in the realms. You could live through peace and joy." I say wistfully, having never really experienced it.

"And wars." Soren points out.

I wave off his negative attitude.

He hikes up his bag and scans the forest.

"We better get moving, it's about a two-week journey to the mountains."

Nodding in agreement, I swing my bag over my shoulder. Turning on my heel, we start walking toward the mountains of Erontil in the north.

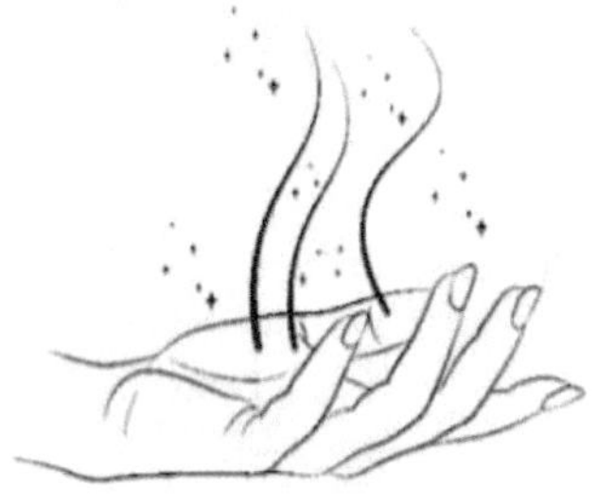

Chapter 8

The first problem occurs two days on the road.

The road seemed to stretch out for miles, putting you in a trance. Then, a black dot appears in the distance. I squint and come to a halt.

Soren stops beside me. "What is it?"

"There's something on the road ahead," I say, not taking my eyes off the mysterious object. He follows my line of sight, squinting.

Soren swears and pulls me deeper into the forest.

"You recognize that? What is it?" I question.

He doesn't answer, he just keeps leading me deeper into the thick trees.

We push through dense foliage and emerge into a large clearing. Finally, he stops and turns to me.

"That's a Ventor. I've only seen them from a distance," he mutters, cursing under his breath.

"What's a Ventor?" I ask, not recalling them from our lessons in Modereo.

"It looks like a giant slug, only it's as fast as a snake and has teeth that can tear through skin as easily as breathing," Soren says grimly.

I swallow hard. "Great. And it's heading right towards us. How do we kill it?"

"No one has ever killed one before."

"No one has ever tried with magic," I wink at him.

He looks at me in disbelief.

I just grin back, but my grin quickly fades as I hear the Ventor's roar.

"Go up onto those rocks over there." I point to a small hill of boulders.

"And leave you here?" he questions.

"Yes." I glance at him, raising my eyebrows. "Unless you're scared for me."

He scoffs and turns his head away.

I smirk. "You care about me, Soren. I feel so honored."

He turns toward the rocks and mutters, "You wish."

I watch him climb up the small hill. Another roar cuts through the air, too close for comfort now.

I turn my head towards the noise and see trees toppling as the Ventor slices its way through the forest. I sink to my knees and press my hands into the soil. Closing my eyes, I sense the creature—about a mile away and gaining fast.

I pull magic from my internal well and send it out toward the Ventor. It senses me and roars in response, picking up its already rapid pace. My power flares with a sense of urgency, and my adrenaline spikes.

I tune out my surroundings and focus on the earth and the Ventor's approach. Vaguely, I hear Soren yelling that it's getting very close, but I ignore him. Instead, I reach out to the surrounding trees, snapping them in half and suspending them in the air. The ground rumbles as I manipulate the earth. I turn the jagged edges toward the clearing in front of me.

Not a second too soon.

The Ventor bursts through the trees, no more than twenty-five feet away. It rears up its head, readying to attack.

I let out a scream as I release my magic, casting through the trees and broken trunks in the air. The makeshift spears impale the Ventor, and its high-pitched screams are enough to make my ears bleed. I take deep breaths and try to move away.

The Ventor collapses forward. It continues to move, wriggling toward me. Blood seeps rapidly out of its wounds. Its dying body seeming to be driven by one final instinct.

I see the long tooth before I feel it. My scream doesn't even sound like my own as I look down and see a long slash across my front. Blood is already pooling around me as I collapse to the side. The long body of the Ventor lying beside me. I try to see if the creature is dead, but my vision blurs, my body numbing from the pain. Darkness tugs at me and I yield to it.

***

Pain ricochets up my back, pulling me from sleep. I try to loosen my stiff body, but when I try to move, my muscles spasm. I blink my eyes open to dim light. I'm in a cave. I see Soren with his back to me, facing the fire.

I push myself up into a sitting position, my body screaming with agony. My breath coming in quick pants from the exertion. Leaning against the cave wall, I try to shake the dizziness away.

Soren turns at the noise. "You're awake," he states, relief evident in his voice. "How are you feeling? It got you pretty good."

I take in his face, the exhaustion clear.

I look down at myself and realize I'm covered in dirt again. I huff out a laugh and wince. "Besides every breath I take being painful, I'm fine. How long have I been out? Is the creature dead?"

"A day and a half," he states. "The bleeding stopped yesterday evening, but you lost a lot of blood. The Ventor is dead. All thanks to you." His tired eyes glint with a touch of pride.

Tension leaves my body at the news and the look in his eyes.

"You should get some rest." I tell him with an apologetic tone.

"I'm fine. I wasn't the one that was almost ripped in half by a giant creature."

I look down at myself and see a tight bandage around the front side of my body. I try to push some healing magic toward it and find my magic is all but depleted. I guess I shouldn't be surprised that killing the Ventor wiped it out.

When I think about how many times I have passed out, I realize he could have left me a long time ago.

"Thank you. For helping me." I say to him sincerely.

"No problem, princess." He responds with a small smile.

A shiver passes through my aching body. I *need to replenish my magic.* I think, somewhat desperately.

"Are there any bodies of water around?" I ask Soren.

He looks at me questioningly. "Yes, there's a small lake about a mile away. Why?"

I answer his question with one of my own. "What do you know about magic and the elements?"

"I know there's four elements, and the Stregoni need to touch their element to successfully wield it. I also know that air is the rarest element, along with someone being able to wield all four."

"That's right. Someone being able to wield three elements is also uncommon. There are only a few of us in Magia, and King Elijah keeps us close. Also, not all Stregoni need to touch their element to wield it; the stronger wielders can use their power simply by willing it. To replenish our magic, being submerged in the elements is the fastest way."

"And you can wield three?" Soren asks slowly, already knowing the answer.

"Yes. I'm a big deal in Magia," I joke with a side grin.

He doesn't laugh with me, staring at me a moment before he responds.

"Impressive." He responds seriously, his mouth curving into a side grin.

I tear my gaze away from his, squashing down the butterflies that flutter from his stare.

I wince as I shift myself to the side. "Let's go to that lake in case we run into any more surprises on the road."

"Hopefully, it doesn't come to that." He frowns. "Can you walk that far?"

I stand up and brace myself against the cave wall as a wave of dizziness passes. "I have no choice. We need to keep moving."

His lips thin. "Fine, at least eat some bread."

I wrinkle my nose. The last thing I want to do is eat.

"You need to eat. You lost a lot of blood."

I sigh at his logic, grabbing the small piece of bread.

I force myself to take small bites, ignoring the nausea. After I finish the whole piece, I feel steadier on my feet. Soren packs up, shouldering both of our bags for the walk to the lake. I shoot him a grateful smile at the gesture.

As we step out of the cave, I squint as the full brightness of the sun hits me. *Bah, I feel like a century old vampire.* Shielding my eyes, I look toward Soren. "Lead the way."

He looks at me and nods, starting at a slow pace. I don't tell him, but I appreciate the speed because each step feels like I'm walking on pins and needles.

My foot catches on a branch, and I tumble forward, righting myself on a tree and taking deep breaths. When I lift my head, Soren is at my side.

"Can you keep going, or do you need a break?"

"I can keep going, I just need a minute."

After several minutes, I start forward again, wincing with each step.

"Oh, for fuck's sake," Soren growls and proceeds to lift me up.

I start to shout in protest, but he cuts me off. "At the pace we are going, it'll take us all afternoon to get there."

I sigh in defeat because he has a good point and relax back into his arms. My body heats up as I become aware of all the areas our bodies are touching. Mentally, I scold myself. *Why am I thinking about him like that? Sure, he's attractive, but he works for that monster. He lives in another world.*

My breathing quickens as my mind turns to how his lips would feel on my skin. How he would feel over top of me, moving in and out—

"Are you alright? You look flushed." Soren's voice pulls me out of my daze.

I clear my throat. "Yes, I'm fine."

My voice still comes out raspy, and he glances my way with an unreadable expression. I look away to clear my head from my temporary insanity of lust and see the lake up ahead. I breathe a big sigh of relief.

We get to the edge of the water, and Soren slowly lowers me down. I look back at him and silently arch my brow. He turns around with a weighted look and gives me privacy to undress. My cheeks redden from his scrutiny. Pivoting towards the water, I hide my reaction before he turns.

I walk into the water until I reach the deepest part. It only goes up to my chest, so I relax my legs and submerge myself. Immediately, I can feel my power coming back, filling me up and giving me a sense of completion. I push it toward my wound and heal myself. My power expands out, taking in the area. A tiny alarm sounds in my mind when it notices another body in the water, moving toward me.

I lift my head out of the water, seeing Soren in the lake with me. An air of unease hangs around us.

"Thought it would be a good time to clean up," he says as he swims closer to me.

A jolt of apprehension goes through me from the intensity in his eyes.

"What are you doing?" I ask cautiously as he approaches.

I don't move away. His eyes flare when I don't retreat.

He stops a few feet away, pausing with an intense look on his face.

"I wasn't sure if I was going to tell you this," he says huskily, "but when your magic was depleted, your mental barrier wasn't up."

It takes me a moment to process his words, my mind going to our walk—all the dirty thoughts I was thinking about him. I feel my cheeks redden, but instead of shying away, I meet his gaze and make a choice.

In my mind, I project a single thought to him: *Are you going to do something about it?*

I snap up my mental barriers as he lets loose a growl and swims toward me. Before I can react, he's already closed the distance.

Our lips crash together, the kiss fierce and unrelenting. There's nothing gentle about it. His hands grip my waist, pulling me flush against him, and heat sparks in my core at the possessiveness of it. I fist my fingers in his hair, tugging him back down to my mouth as if I can't get enough.

"I still hate you," he mutters against my lips.

"Right back at you," I breathe out. Hate being the furthest thing I'm feeling right now.

A sharp gasp escapes me as he wraps a hand around my hair and tugs my head back, exposing my throat. I let him, tilting my head to the side—offering him that control. His mouth is on my neck before I can second-guess myself, his lips brushing my skin with dangerous intent.

My breath hitches when his fingers slide against me, plunging in with an expertise that has my body arching instinctively. He watches me, his eyes dark with hunger.

"So beautiful," he murmurs, voice rough with want.

The tension coils in my stomach as he watches my body reacting, moving in deliberate strokes, pushing me closer and closer to the edge. He pumps his fingers in and out of me, adding a third, stretching me. Then, just before I shatter, he withdraws his fingers. I whimper at the loss. He smirks at my reaction.

Leaning in, he whispers against my ear, "I want you to come around my dick, princess. I want to watch you fall apart with me inside you."

A shiver racks my body, and before I can process his words, I gasp, feeling him line himself up with my entrance.

He pushes in, slow and deliberate, and for a moment, we both go still, breathing heavily as we adjust to each other.

Slowly, I start to move, he groans as he grabs my hips and starts pounding into me as he matches my tempo.

Water ripples around us as we fuck and lose ourselves in rhythm.

I glance down, watching us move, over and over, coming together and falling apart. My head tips back, and his mouth finds my throat again. His lips leaving a trail of fire across my skin.

The pressure builds inside me, tightening with every thrust.

"I'm close," I pant.

His pace quickens, driving into me. He starts pounding faster and harder, until pleasure explodes through me, blinding in its intensity. He follows a heartbeat later, a curse slipping past his lips as he shudders against me. We both look at each other for a moment, neither of us speaks.

Eventually, he pulls back, running a hand through his wet hair.

"Damn it," I mutter, breathless. "Of course, you'd be good at that." I say with a grumble.

His lips curl into a cocky smirk. "You weren't so bad yourself, princess."

We make our way to the shore in comfortable silence, grabbing our pile of clothes and dressing with our backs to one another.

"Has your power come back?" Soren asks as he fastens his belt. A softness in his gaze that wasn't there before.

Pushing down the hope flickering, I shoot him a small smile.

Flexing my fingers, I test the magic humming beneath my skin. "As full as it can be right now," I say, though there's a strange hollowness in my chest.

"Good." He nods. "Then let's keep moving."

My lips twitch at his diligence as I follow him.

We start walking through the forest toward Erontil, but this time, something feels different.

Chapter 9

A day passes without incident, then another. On the third day, the forest seems to take on an eerie air. The wind whistles sharply between the overgrown bushes. My instincts flicker, but I ignore them, not sensing anything dangerous.

The bad feeling doesn't go away as we walk. Then, I hear a rustling of leaves. We grind to a halt, trying to discern whether it's an animal or human.

A sharp whistle sounds and guards jump out. Surrounding us.

Both of us freeze, caught off guard that they've managed to track us so easily.

Then we recover. Swords clash as we meet their attack head-on. I quickly scan the scene—there are too many of them for me to waste time in direct combat. I step back, sheathing my sword and drawing my daggers instead.

Whipping out my daggers, I turn to the side as I hear a rustling sound to my left. I pivot just as another guard crashes through the trees.

I let my dagger fly and turn to my next target, briefly hearing the thud of it.

I barely have time to register the kill before I see another threat—one that makes my blood run cold.

Time seems to slow as a guard creeps up behind Soren. My heart stutters as he raises his sword.

I hurl my second dagger, praying that it's faster than a sword. It sinks deep into the man's back just as he's about to strike. Soren turns, eyes flicking to the fallen guard before meeting mine. When I see he's okay, a breath I didn't know I was holding escapes me. A quick nod of gratitude is all he has time to give before we're both forced back into the fight.

But I don't hear the next enemy sneaking up behind me.

Soren shouts a warning—too late. A sharp, searing pain rakes across my back. I hiss and spin, another dagger already in hand. I strike fast, ramming the blade into my attacker's chest. His weight sags against me, blood soaking my fingers as I twist the dagger deeper. With a grunt, I shove him off and let his body hit the ground.

Silence falls.

The last of the guards are down. I hear a soft thud. I take a shaky breath and turn—just in time to see Soren drop to his knees, clutching his arm.

I wipe my blade clean and hurry over to him. My back burns from the rapid movement. Fortunately for me, it's a shallow cut.

"How bad is it?" I ask, kneeling beside him. He presses on the wound, blood trickling between his fingers.

"They got me pretty deep," he mutters. "I'll be fine though." Each word he speaks sounds laced with pain.

I shoot him a doubtful look.

"I could ask you the same thing," he says pointedly, nodding toward my back.

"I'm fine." I say to him and walk stiffly towards our supplies. My back throbs with each step I take. The blood drips from the wound, splattering onto the dry leaves.

I wordlessly point to the log and raise my eyebrow at him. "Sit." Surprisingly, he listens and goes to sit on it. Soren watches as I grab the water. I head back to him and crouch down. Inhaling sharply from the movement. When I pour the water over his wound, he hisses quietly. Without a word, I rip a strip of fabric from the bottom of my shirt, wrapping his arm. While I'm doing this, I can feel his gaze on me. I ignore it at first, focusing on treating the wound. *You're just dressing a wound, Adira. Why does it feel so intimate?* I ask myself.

The weight of his gaze causes me to look up. His eyes convey a deeper feeling. Something I am not willing to think about right now.

"There. Now you won't be bleeding all over the place," I say once I'm done, doing my best to ignore the stinging pain along my spine.

Soren exhales and shifts, glancing at me. "Thanks," he murmurs softly.

Then he clears his throat and gestures at me.

"Are you sure you can walk?" Worry lines his forehead.

I roll my eyes, making light of the situation. "I've survived worse. A little scratch on my back is nothing."

I go to stand, my movements jerky from the stiffness of my body. I give him a smile that feels more like a wince.

His brows pull together. "Why can't you just heal yourself?"

I frown. "My magic is depleting. I need to conserve it in case we run into any more surprises on the road."

Soren considers that, then nods. "Alright. But we should move. Someone's bound to come looking for these guards." He pushes to his feet with only a slight wince.

I narrow my eyes at him. "Are you sure you can travel so soon?" I pointedly look at his arm—it's already starting to bleed through the bandage.

He smirks. "Like someone once told me, we don't have a choice."

I shake my head, biting back a smile as he throws my own words back at me.

"Come on, wise ass," I say, stepping forward and doing my best to ignore the sharp sting of my wound.

We start to turn back toward the path; I twist too sharply. Pain steals my breath. I lean against a tree as it slowly fades back to a dull throb.

"I'm okay." I say before Soren can ask. "Let's go."

He has a doubtful expression on his face, but doesn't argue.

We leave behind the now tarnished area. The bitter smell of copper lingering in the air. Acting as a beacon for the predators of the forest.

***

We walk in silence through the dense trees. I trudge along, keeping my breathing even. I notice Soren adjusts his pace to match mine. A smile threatens to show at the display of thoughtfulness.

Halfway through the day, Soren breaks the silence.

"What's Modereo like?"

"It's incredible." My voice softens at the thought of home. "The air hums with magic, and every breath feels cleaner. We have creatures that roam free, and our castle floats in the sky."

"Do you miss it?"

"I do." I admit. "I miss the constant buzz of magic. I miss the vibrant people. I miss the way the sky changes color as the sun sinks below the mountains."

"Hopefully we can remove that Vormr then." Soren responds with a thin smile.

"Hopefully." I echo back.

I peek over at him. "You should see it for yourself." As soon as I speak the words, I realize how much I want to show him my realm.

He holds my gaze, something unreadable flickering in his expression.

"Maybe one day I can." He says tentatively.

His brows furrow like he's about to say something else, but he stops himself and shakes his head. His eyes linger on me a moment before he asks, "Do you know anyone with the ability to wield air?"

Strange question to get caught up on. I think with my head tilted to the side as I regard him.

"Not personally. I've heard of three Stregoni who could wield all four elements, but they were taken to the castle for 'special training'... and never seen again."

"That's never a good sign."

"No, it isn't," I murmur.

"Have you ever thought about looking for them?"

I hesitate. "I have, but... it's just too dangerous for me."

"For you?"

I stiffen. "I mean, for everyone." I quickly correct, my power rises with my panic. A gust of wind whips my hair back. I eye Soren nervously, but he seems lost in thought, not noticing the abrupt change in weather.

I might be starting to trust him, but that doesn't mean I need to tell him everything.

The memory of my sixteenth birthday surfaces unbidden.

I had woken up excited to practice magic. I already had control over earth, water, and fire, and I was eager to push my limits. The room was still dark with the curtains drawn, but as soon as I sat up, my body buzzed with a strange anticipation. Before I could swing my legs over the side of the bed—

The windows exploded inward.

Glass rained down, curtains ripped away, and wind howled through the room. I froze, heart hammering in my chest. My mother burst through the door, her eyes scanning the wreckage before landing on me.

"What happened?" she asked, but I was too stunned to respond.

She took in the broken glass and the restless energy crackling around me and nodded, as if she had expected this.

"Listen to me, Adira. You are okay. I knew this was going to happen."

I whipped my head toward her at that. "You knew?"

She met my gaze, calm and certain. "Yes. I knew you'd need all four elements. You are special. You're going to transform the world someday." My mother cryptically tells me. I feel my face tighten in confusion but before I can ask further questions, she cuts me off, "You have to hide this fourth element. If anyone finds out you can wield all four, you will be in danger." Her expression hardened. "I will train you to control it, but you mustn't tell anyone. Okay? Do you understand?"

I agreed with her. From that day forward, she pushed me harder than ever.

I shake off the memory, focusing on the air around me. It feels heavy tonight, but I let it hum in my veins, strengthening me as much as it can.

Up ahead, Soren slows and sets his pack down.

Without turning to me, he says, "We should eat something before we keep going."

I hadn't realized how hungry I was until he mentioned it.

Pulling out a piece of bread, I spot a bush nearby, its branches heavy with berries. I pluck a few and rub one against my forearm, waiting for a reaction. No tingling. They're safe.

I gather a handful and return to the log where Soren is sitting. Holding out my palm, I offer him some berries.

He glances at me before taking them. "Thanks."

"No problem." I worry how much it's true. Two weeks ago, I would have let him starve. *But would you have?* My internal voice asks knowingly. *Nope. Not going to think about that.*

We eat our berries in companionable silence. The only sound is the birds chirping while the wind rustles the leaves.

He digs into his pack and pulls out a strip of jerky, extending it toward me. "I noticed you were out." His voice is gruff, but there's something thoughtful in the gesture.

I hesitate a moment before taking it. Surprise colors my tone. "Thanks, Soren."

His lips twitch. "Anytime, princess."

I try not to dwell on the fact that I don't hate the nickname anymore.

Chapter 10

We manage to get four days out from Erontil when a strange feeling washes over me. Almost as if we are being watched. I scan the area with my magic, but sense nothing. I attempt to shrug it off as we keep moving, but the feeling lingers for most of the day.

My body is tense from hours of alertness. If Soren picks up on my agitation, he doesn't say anything. *Maybe he can't sense anything unusual. Maybe I'm going insane.*

Just as that thought appears, a heavy awareness settles over me.

Scanning the area, I feel a small presence near us.

I put my hand out to stop Soren, feeling a twinge of lingering pain from my back wound. He doesn't hesitate as he reaches to pull out his sword. I stop him before he gets the blade halfway out of the sheath. I feel his questioning gaze.

I walk ahead into the clearing. "Child, you can come out. We won't harm you," I say in my softest voice.

A full minute passes before we see a dirty child with long blonde hair stick her head out from behind a tree.

Soren instinctively steps in front of me.

I hear a slight inhale from him as the child walks further into view. Stepping around him, I ignore his warning look.

"Hi there, my name is Adira. What's your name?"

A soft whisper of an answer comes from the child. "Poderosa."

"Poderosa, what a beautiful name. Did you know that means powerful? You must be very brave to be out here on your own. How old are you?"

"I'm ten," she replies, taking a cautious step closer to us.

I take a tentative step toward her. "Ten! Wow, so grown up. This is my friend Soren."

He raises an eyebrow at the word *friend*, muttering something under his breath.

He waves from the edge of the clearing. "Nice to meet you, Poderosa."

She moves to hide behind me. "Bad man," she says and grabs my shirt. A flash of hurt crosses his face before he covers the emotion with an easy smile.

"No, Soren is a good man. I promise," I crouch down to tell her, thinking it's scary how much I'm starting to believe my own words.

She immediately wraps her arms around my neck to be carried. Bracing myself for the pain, I stand with her in my arms, my back burning with the effort. I force a neutral expression, so Soren doesn't notice.

"Do you have any parents?" I ask. She shakes her head side to side. The movement causes my back to spasm. I twist to hide it.

I share a glance with Soren, both of us knowing we can't leave this child here.

"Well, Soren and I are going on an adventure. Would you like to come with us?"

Poderosa nods and tightens her grip on me.

I look over at Soren again. "I guess we have a traveling companion."

We keep moving and manage to avoid any more surprises. Nightfall creeps up on us, and we choose a secluded cave to make camp.

Normally, we wouldn't risk a fire, but the child is shaking from the cold, so Soren goes to gather some wood. While he's gone, I pull out some bread from my pack.

I hand it over to Poderosa, and she devours it in seconds.

I hear a rustling near the entrance of the cave and turn, locking eyes with Soren, both of ours reflecting sadness.

Soren sets the logs up, and I summon my fire magic to the surface. I will the logs to catch flame and notice Soren's gaping mouth.

He stares at the dancing flames for a moment. I can see his thoughts swirling in his eyes.

"You didn't need to touch the element," he states obviously.

I look into his eyes. "No, I didn't."

I watch as he realizes the unspoken words, and his eyes widen slightly, but he doesn't say anything. *Yes, Soren. I am powerful.* I give him a side glance to stop any further questions. I don't want to lie to him, and I'm not ready to tell him my secrets.

Shortly after Poderosa eats some stew, she falls fast asleep by the fire. Soren and I sit around finishing our portions.

"I can't believe people can just neglect children like this. It's so upsetting," I say with barely concealed anger.

Soren sighs. "This is a common occurrence in our world, unfortunately."

"It's terrible," I mutter while tugging the blanket up to her chin.

"You're good with her," Soren says with a touch of surprise in his voice.

"Why do you seem so surprised?" I scoff.

"Well, you aren't exactly the best example for motherhood," Soren responds.

Before I can ask why, he conveys his opinion to me. "You're reckless, mouthy, and you don't blink twice when you kill someone."

His words sting, but I don't show him that.

"Damn, don't hold back," I say with mock offense.

I sigh. "But you aren't wrong. You can blame my mother for all that."

"Your mother? Why?" he asks.

I take a deep breath and look over at him through the orange flames. "She was peculiar," I start.

"She seemed to have it in her head that I was special," I say with a rough laugh. "And since I was special, I had to be prepared. You can start to come into your power around ages fourteen to sixteen and reach full power by age eighteen. But she started training me long before I was fourteen. At first, it was normal—extra training with all the weapons you can imagine. Then, she decided I needed to be efficient with both hands. So she would tie my right hand to a tree and attack me, forcing me to use my left hand. At first, I didn't think she'd actually injure me. I was wrong. I remember the shock I felt when she first drew blood. I confided in my friends at school, thinking they were receiving the same lessons. They looked at me with a mixture of confusion and concern. Then, when I started to show power, it got stranger."

I pause as my mind drifts back.

"Strange how?" Soren's voice brings me back to the present.

"Strange like tying a rock to my leg and tossing me in a lake. My only instruction was to manipulate the water to keep myself alive. I became well acquainted with panic at a young age. The feeling of your lungs burning and not a flicker of power aiding you is terrifying. One I will never forget. Fortunately, my magic did respond. Right when I was on the precipice of giving up." I pause as those dark feelings swarm back into me. "She would also make me eat poison until I developed an immunity to small doses. I wouldn't only be tested through normal trials; she would sporadically poison some of my meals. I became scared of eating, not knowing which food was going to send me to the toilet. That was a rough month," I say hoarsely.

"It was stuff like that. And after each near-death experience, when I was well enough to yell at her, she would tell me it was for my own good, that I'd thank her someday. That it was for the greater good," I finish scornfully.

"Well, I wasn't expecting that," Soren says bluntly after a moment.

I chuckle at his abruptness, looking up to meet his gaze, relieved when I don't see any pity in his eyes.

We sit in silence, watching the fire crackle for a while until I decide to break it.

"I can take the first watch tonight."

Soren shakes his head. "You need the sleep."

"One of the things my mother made me do was learn to stay awake for days and still be alert. I'll be fine for the first watch. Plus, you need to heal that arm, pretty boy, just in case we need your big muscles again." I smirk.

He rolls his eyes. "Fine. Wake me up in a few hours," he says tiredly.

"I will. Night."

Not long after he lays down, his breathing evens out.

I place my hands on the cave floor, drawing in the excess energy stored within the rock. Caves are powerful energy sources that strengthen your magic. They are natural reservoirs where the universe's power lingers, absorbed by stone and hidden in the dark caverns.

Quietly, I move to Soren and place my hands on his wounded arm. Murmuring a few incantations, I channel magic into his injury, strengthening the spell to speed his healing. A small trickle of power moves to my back, mending my own wound.

Swaying slightly, I stand and return to the other side of the fire. Normally, this level of healing wouldn't even make a dent in my reserves—especially in a cave.

I prop myself against the wall, letting my mind wander on the journey to come.

Will we be able to find the goddesses, complete both of our tasks, and locate Claude—all while taking care of a child? I can't even fathom how hard the next few weeks will be. Hopefully, my magic doesn't weaken too much more, or—

A small movement startles me. Poderosa snuggles up against me, and my heart clenches painfully at the thought of what this child has had to endure.

I stroke her hair and release the smallest pulse of magic to soothe her.

***

I wake Soren up close to dawn.

"It's almost sunup, why didn't you wake me earlier?" He argues angrily.

I just shrug.

"You needed the sleep more than I did. The cave recharges me anyhow, I just need an hour to rest and then I'll be fine."

I lay my head down and just as I am about to fade away, I hear "thanks for healing my arm" in a low voice.

I feel myself smile as I fall into a deep sleep.

***

I wake feeling better than I have in days. I look down and notice that Poderosa is still curled up against me.

"Poderosa," I say softly, "wake up."

She jerks awake, her breaths coming fast and shallow.

I pull her into a tight hug. "It's okay. Calm down, you're safe."

She clings to me, her small body trembling. After a few minutes, her heart rate slows, and her breathing evens out.

"I had a scary dream," she whispers.

"Oh no. Do you want to tell me about it?"

She takes a deep breath. "There was a scary monster, and it came from the water. It attacked all of us."

Soren steps into the cave, his voice light. "Don't worry. I won't let any scary monster get us."

I glance over at him, then shift my attention back to the task at hand. "We should get moving. We don't want to waste daylight."

I start to help pack up, but Poderosa won't loosen her grip on me.

Soren huffs a quiet laugh and goes to disassemble our campsite himself.

Before leaving, I place my hands on the cave floor one last time, drawing in the energy stored in the stone and locking it into my reserve.

When I stand, Soren is ready to go.

We step out into the sunlight and continue on north.

***

We are a day out from the bottom of the mountains of Erontil when we come upon a large lake.

We decide to stop and wash off, but as we near the water's edge, Poderosa starts panicking.

I stop in my tracks. "What's wrong?"

"Bad water. Monster."

I remember her nightmare and crouch down to her level, trying to calm her down.

"It's alright, Poderosa. There's no monster in here."

"That's right. I'll walk in, and you'll see." Soren steps closer to the water.

Just as his foot touches the edge, a low rumbling shakes the ground.

We instinctively reach for our weapons, my muscles tense in preparation. We look at each other, slipping into our fighting stances.

The water explodes upward, and an enormous, black, eel-like creature emerges, breaking the tension of the water's surface.

It rises fourteen feet into the air, hissing, its terrifying mouth gaping open. It has no teeth, just a long, razor-sharp tongue dripping with purple acid.

I summon a wall of stone between us and the beast, then turn and run toward the tree line.

It only buys us a second. The creature bursts through the stone barrier as if it were nothing.

I put Poderosa down. "Run," I tell her.

She takes off, disappearing deeper into the forest.

The creature lunges at us, knocking down trees as if they're twigs.

Soren moves first, slicing into its side. The monster screeches and turns its attention to him.

I take the opening. Pressing my hands into the ground, I summon my magic.

"Ego praecipio tibi tardus," I whisper.

The massive eel slows to a crawl.

Soren charges in, hacking at its neck. It takes several swings, but finally, the eel's head separates from its body, crashing to the forest floor with a loud thud.

I release my spell.

The eel's body spasms violently. Its strong tail whips out, snapping a tree in half.

The trunk tilts—falling straight toward me.

My limbs feel sluggish from magic exhaustion. I try to move, but my legs won't cooperate.

At the last second, Soren tackles me, rolling us both out of the way. The tree crashes down beside us, shaking the earth.

When we stop rolling, Soren lands on top of me, panting from the rush of adrenaline.

Our eyes lock. The air between us shifts, charged with something unspoken. A speck of dirt draws my attention, I reach out, brushing it off his cheek. My breath hitches as his eyes darken.

Fuck it. We almost died. Who cares about what may or may not happen?

We both start leaning in—

"You're alive!" a tiny voice exclaims.

Soren's jaw clenches at the interruption. He quickly pulls away, clearly frustrated.

"We're okay." I say just as Poderosa throws herself into my arms, knocking me flat onto my back.

I chuckle at her enthusiasm, but then the realization strikes me.

I look down at her. "Did you see this happen in your nightmare?" I ask in disbelief.

She nods solemnly. "Yes, but I didn't see you stop it."

I share a look with Soren.

"Poderosa, that's incredible. Have you always been able to do this?"

"Yes." She nods.

Later that night, after Poderosa is fast asleep, Soren and I walk a short distance away from the campsite to talk about what happened.

"I've never heard of anything like that. Have you?" Soren asks.

"No, I haven't. It sounds like she has seer powers, but there hasn't been a seer in centuries." I ponder.

"Maybe she has a hybrid of powers. She must be from your world," he suggests. "Now that I think about it, I can't read her mind. It's almost like she has a block up. Could that mean her powers are similar to yours?"

"No. I've never heard of anything like that before. Premonitions are only for seers, gods, or goddesses."

We both glance back at her.

"Whoever she is, she's special," I say firmly. "And she stumbled upon us." I express fiercely.

"We need to protect her."

Soren hesitates a moment then nods.

"I agree." He says, the surprise evident in his voice. "No matter who she is, we can't leave her defenseless." Soren ends with a note of finality.

I hide my smile at his willingness to do anything for the child.

He clears his throat. "As much as it pains me to say this, we were a pretty good team today."

"We were." I think about how lucky it was that no one got hurt.

"Thank you for saving my life," I grumble.

"It's only fair, since you've saved mine so many times," he admits reluctantly.

I smirk. "I guess we're even then."

He huffs a laugh, the corner of his mouth twitching. "I guess so."

We lock eyes, my mind replays the earlier scene. His eyes narrow in interest as blood rushes to my face.

I take a step back, turning my attention to the tree line.

"Now go get some sleep. I'll take the first watch."

I glance over at him as he speaks.

Noticing my look, he adds, "Don't worry. I promise to wake you for your turn."

"Okay," I sigh in defeat, already feeling the heaviness of the day settling into my limbs.

I lie down next to Poderosa, and Soren stretches out beside me, his back resting against a fallen tree.

I blurt out a question that's been nagging at me since I met Soren.

"Where were you when your family was killed?"

He doesn't say anything for a moment, and I internally wince, realizing too late that I might have crossed a line. Just as I'm about to backtrack, pretending I never asked, he speaks.

"I was in the forest, gathering wood for our fire," he starts quietly.

"It was my brother's turn to do it, but he was pretending he hurt his leg to get out of it. I was so mad at him because it was cold that day—snow had fallen earlier that morning. I called him a liar and trudged out."

"When I got back later that evening, the door was hanging sideways on one hinge. I managed to push it open even though my hands were shaking."

"There was blood everywhere. The guards hadn't been gentle."

He swallows hard.

"Before I could even process it, I heard footsteps behind me. I turned and saw four guards coming my way. I tried to run, but they caught up to me easily."

"They took me to the King. He tried to justify it to me—said it was my family's fault. That they were working with the rebellion. He said I had to swear loyalty to him or die."

"My only thought was revenge. So, I swore my allegiance and was thrown into training. Turns out, I was good at it."

"The first thing I did was find out who killed my family. And I ended their lives."

Soren says it simply, but the weight of it lingers in the air between us.

"The King was angry. He threw me in solitary for a week."

"When I got out, I pretended I was okay with everything. But I spent every moment researching ways to break a blood oath—ways to kill him."

"Eventually, he realized I was one of the best. He appointed me his assassin."

"I had no choice but to take it."

"Looking that monster in the face every day is the punishment I deserve for not being there to protect my family."

"All the people I kill mark my soul, but that's the burden I have to carry so I can avenge them."

A flash of irrational anger fills me as I think about what he's done for the King.

He never had a choice.

My heart feels heavy for him.

"You were just a kid," I say softly. "You couldn't have stopped what happened."

"I guess we'll never know." His voice is grim, final.

"Get some sleep, Adira. I'll wake you when it's your turn."

Sensing he won't say anything else, I turn onto my side.

No wonder he was so somber when we first set out on this journey.

I briefly close my eyes and vow to myself that I won't let him lose anything else.

***

Soren wakes me sometime later. After our heavy conversation last night, I feel a lingering tension hanging between us.

"I'm going to do a quick check of the area," I say, knowing full well he's aware I could just use my magic to scan the forest for miles.

He doesn't respond as I get up and wander away from the campsite. The moment I step away from the fire, the crisp night air clears my head.

When I return, Soren has turned onto his side, already asleep.

I let out a sigh of frustration.

Why am I attracted to the enemy? It's so foolish. But then again—is he really the enemy? His life isn't his own to control.

Okay, Adira, think of all the reasons you can't stand him.

My thoughts consume me for the rest of my watch, but I can't deny the pull I feel toward him—the constant awareness of him.

I shake my head with a sigh and force myself to focus on the surrounding forest.

Soon, the sun begins to rise. Soren and Poderosa wake, and we have a quick breakfast.

All we have left is some stale bread and berries, but we make do.

Excitement and nervous energy swirl around us.

Today, we will reach the mountains of Erontil.

Chapter 11

Around sunset, we reach the base of the mountains.

"Apparently, there's a secret path that needs to be revealed to you," I say, glancing around the dense forest.

"Well, how do we reveal it?"

I roll my eyes. "If I knew how, I'd do it. Let's look around."

Soren chuckles. "Smartass."

We start searching—checking caves, looking behind trees. As we move farther alongside the mountain, we stumble into a breathtaking clearing, where thick vines drape over the entire area.

Soren starts hacking through the vines, clearly frustrated.

Poderosa's eyes dart around the area. She nervously whispers to me. "I feel something watching us."

I pause my search at her confession. Closing my eyes, I will my magic up, it expands through the area. I sense nothing. Then, a whisper of unknown eather caresses my power. I hesitate for a moment, unsure if it's a trap.

Pushing through my doubts, I yield to the mysterious source, letting it grasp onto my magic. My power shifts and a low pulse tugs at my chest. I follow the feeling to where Soren is cutting through vines.

"Stop." I tell him.

"What?" He asks as he turns, the frustration clear in his voice.

The pull of energy vibrates beneath my skin.

"It's here. Behind the vines," I say with barely hidden anticipation.

Soren doesn't question me and immediately gets back to work, pushing aside the thick greenery. Poderosa stays close behind me.

"Powerful," she whispers.

I turn to her. "There's an old magic in this place. That must be what you're feeling."

Soren pulls out his sword, cutting through a thick section of vines. He parts the loose pieces, revealing a thin, narrow cave entrance.

The unfamiliar power retreats. Slinking deep into the cave.

Cautiously, we move forward. Soren takes the lead, already slipping into his fighting stance.

The tight passage opens into a vast cavern, at the center of which stands a stone altar. The scent of damp stone mixed with old magic clings to my nose as we walk deeper. When we step inside, the lanterns lining the walls flicker to life, casting an eerie red glow over the space. The air in the large space feels charged with an uneasy energy.

On the altar lies a single page of magically preserved paper. We step closer to it. The lanterns flickering ominously when we do. The deep red light making it difficult to see.

I reach my hand out to the altar, but Soren stops me.

"This could be a trap." He says, eyes scanning the space.

"Or," I reply, "it could be a test."

Before he can respond, I reassure him. "I don't sense anything wrong here."

He mutters something about me being too optimistic but releases his hold on my arm. Turning my attention back to the altar, I reach for it.

As soon as my hand touches the altar, the words jumble on the page. I jump in shock as my power is pricked. The air fills with harsh whispers before it quiets. My eyes fly back to the page. It flashes a bright white light, obscuring my vision. When the light clears, the words are legible.

Shaking away the strangeness, I read the passage aloud:

Three tasks, and then you shall ask.

Only one must complete all.

First, find Eira's mark. To start, one must look in the dark.

Second, search in the lost cave to reveal the message of Orlo.

Third, enter the Chambers of Harnew and come out on the other side.

As soon as I finish reading, a tingle runs through my body, ending at my fingertips. It bursts out. The charged air shifts, leaving behind a grim atmosphere. I ignore the way the change feels like it is signaling what is to come.

Soren and I exchange bleak glances.

"Do you know these tales?" I ask.

"Not all of them. King Dahak withheld stories about powerful beings," he replies.

"So the first task deals with Eira's mark... No one has even come close to finding it."

"Then how do we know it even exists? What if this is just another legend?" He questions skeptically.

I just shrug, not having an answer.

He sighs, running his hand through his hair.

"Okay, let's hear the story. Hopefully there will be a clue in it."

Settling onto the stone floor, I begin the tale.

It all started in a small village east of here, where a poor family lived. That didn't stop their youngest child, Eira, from being the sweetest girl. Everyone in the village loved her.

She would pick flowers and hand them out, going door to door to bring joy to her neighbors.

One evening, a wolf wandered into the village and attacked Eira. She was only ten years old. As she lay dying, the entire village gathered. Holding hands, they formed a circle around the little dying girl and used their magic to heal her.

They had never performed a spell this powerful before. Their magic, combined, surged beyond anything they had ever controlled. When they released it into Eira, it didn't just save her—it changed her. She became more powerful than any of them.

A few resented this, but most simply loved her for who she was. She remained kind and sweet, selfless, and eager to help.

On her eighteenth birthday, her full awakening arrived. The surge of power within her was unlike anything the village had ever seen. It drew the attention of Sybil—another girl in the village, one who had been prophesied to be the strongest Stregona. Sybil's heart twisted with jealousy.

Eira suspected something was amiss when she caught Sybil watching her, whispering to others in the shadows. What Eira didn't know was that Sybil had discovered an ancient legend—one that spoke of a sacred ground that could amplify one's power under a full moon... or strip it away completely.

Eira grew even more suspicious of Sybil and quickly learned that she was trying to take her power. The whispers at school reached Eira's ears, confirming her suspicions. Eira didn't know when or where Sybil would strike. But one night after she was walking home, a magic tie that suppresses one's power was wrapped around her arms. She passed out from the immediate disappearance of her magic. When she awoke, she was tied to a tree, her magic still gone.

Sybil stood before her, already casting the spell.

Eira fought against the bonds, her strength weakening by the second. She snapped free just as Sybil uttered the final words. Her magic slowly streaming back into her.

With every ounce of energy she had left, Eira thrust her power out and met it halfway. There was an explosion of raw power outward. The night exploded in a blinding light as they both pushed all their energy towards each other.

But Eira could feel it—her strength was draining too fast; she knew she couldn't let Sybil take her powers. Sybil's spell was changing her. If she succeeded, she wouldn't just take Eira's magic—she would become something else entirely. Eira knew she could not let that happen. The people of the village did not deserve a fate like that to befall them.

There was only one choice.

She only hesitated for a moment, wishing there was another way. Her heart heavy with what was to come.

Eira recalled a forbidden spell, one whispered of in old texts, one never to be used. A spell that would return her magic to the universe itself.

She whispered it under her breath, raised her hands to the sky—

And let it go.

As the last of her magic left her body, Sybil's spell struck her chest.

She died instantly.

The villagers mourned her at first. Then they came to celebrate her sacrifice. Never forgetting what she did.

"To this day, there's rumored to be a spot in the ground where Eira sacrificed herself and her powers so Sybil wouldn't become a monster.

She was always wicked, but Eira tried to keep her from gaining the power to destroy. I've searched for more information, but I've had no luck," I remark.

Soren smirks and winks. "Well, sweetheart, you've never had me."

I raise an eyebrow, eyeing him skeptically, ignoring the tingle that runs up my spine when he calls me sweetheart.

A bit of redness must trickle into my cheeks because he takes note of my reaction, smirking wider.

"With your magic senses and my tracking, we should have no trouble finding it," he declares confidently.

I feel a tug at my sleeve and look down at Poderosa.

She leads me to the cave entrance, parting the vines.

"Creek," she says, pointing southeast.

I squat to her level. "What's at the creek?"

She looks directly into my eyes. "Eira."

Soren lets out a low whistle. "Well, I guess you don't need me. You just need this smart girl," he says, winking playfully at Poderosa.

She blushes under his attention.

I can't shake the feeling that stumbling upon Poderosa wasn't just luck. My mother's voice echoes in my head, *there's no such thing as coincidences, Adira. Everything happens for a reason.*

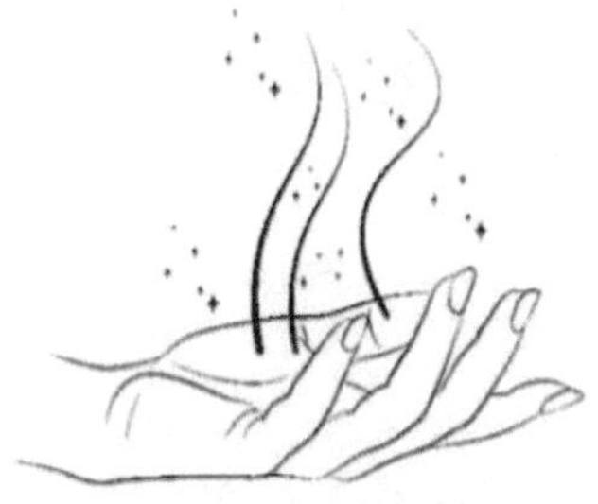

Chapter 12

We've been walking toward the southeast for about a day when Soren suddenly puts out his hand, signaling us to stop. He crouches low, his entire body going tense.

My pulse quickens as I instinctively go on high alert.

"What?" I whisper.

He doesn't take his eyes off a spot to our left. His muscles coil, fingers twitching toward his sword, before shifting to his dagger.

A prickle of unease runs down my spine at his tenseness.

"Dinner." He answers.

In one fluid motion, he pulls his dagger from its sheath. He pauses, taking in the stillness of the forest. Then, he hurls the dagger twenty feet forward. It cuts through layers of trees, disappearing into the dense forest. A moment later, I hear a sharp thunk—the unmistakable sound of a small body hitting the ground.

We walk toward the noise and find a rabbit pierced clean through the eye.

My eyes widen at the sheer accuracy of his throw. Soren smirks at my reaction.

"I didn't become the King's number one assassin with no skills."

"I guess not," I mutter, feeling an unexpected heat spark inside me at the display.

Soren retrieves the rabbit and finds a fallen log to sit on. Without hesitation, he begins skinning it.

Well, I can't let him have all the fun. I think to myself.

I listen carefully to the forest and whip out my dagger. I hear another rabbit about thirty feet to my left. In one swift motion, I spin and release my weapon. A thud echoes through the trees.

Following the sound, I find my dagger embedded directly into another rabbit's right eye.

Silently, I return to our makeshift camp and begin setting up a fire, motioning for Poderosa to gather some sticks.

Soren eyes the rabbit in my hands, doubt in his gaze.

"And this was from thirty feet away." I hum to him as I start skinning it.

"You obviously used your magic." He scoffs.

"Actually, I didn't. I'm just that skilled too." I say with a smirk.

He grumbles under his breath, "beginner's luck."

I scoff in amusement, flicking dirt at him.

He chuckles at the childish display, raising his hands in mock defense.

"Okay. That was quite impressive, princess." He grudgingly admits.

"I know." I reply confidently.

Shaking his head at my response, he chuckles lightly.

The sound of crunching leaves pulls our attention to the edge of the tree line. Poderosa returns with an armful of sticks.

Once the fire is crackling and we settle down to eat. Soren distributes the food. Leaning toward me, he grabs his water skin. As he pulls back, his fingers brush my knee. I jolt at the simple touch. He shoots me a knowing smile. *Seriously, Adira? He barely touched you. Pull it together. Modereo is counting on you.*

As we eat, I notice Poderosa playing with her food, glancing between Soren and I. She moves closer, her small hands twisting in her lap.

"I was taken by bad men," she starts shakily.

I reach for her hand and silently encourage her to keep going.

She hesitates, rubbing her arms in comfort.

"They took me to a dark place underground," she continues. "They made me tell them what was going to happen before it happened. But I couldn't always guess right... and when I didn't, they hit me." Her voice falters. "It happened a lot. When I got it right, I got to sleep in the bed."

My stomach clenches. A wave of protectiveness fills me.

She falters, looking between us for reassurance. I give her what I hope is an encouraging smile. Silently urging her to finish the story, despite my rising anger.

"I don't know how long I was there," she murmurs, touching her hair. "But when they took me, my hair was here." She points just below her chin. "I remember being so scared."

My fists tighten in anger. Her hair has grown at least nine inches.

She was held captive for over a year.

"One day, one of the bad men was drinking and forgot to lock the door properly. I managed to sneak out while they were sleeping. I walked for a long time—maybe a week—before I ran into you both." Her voice is barely a whisper now.

I pull her into a hug. "You are so brave. Those men will never hurt you again. We'll protect you. Right, Soren?" I ask with a soft voice, already knowing his answer.

"That's right, Poderosa." His voice gentler than usual.

"Don't even think about those bad men anymore. They can't hurt you." He says with certainty, seeming to speak to the both of them. My heart softens for them both. The defenses I built up as a child falling more and more each day.

She lets out a soft sigh and curls up between us. Shortly after, she drifts off to sleep.

I stare into the fire, watching the flames dance.

"Nine inches," I say quietly. "That's well over a year, at least. I wonder who took her."

"Not sure. Unfortunately, there are lots of people who would do that. It's a horrible world we live in." Soren responds with a resigned sigh.

"I don't like to think of it that way," I murmur.

He turns to me. "What do you mean?"

"There's a lot of bad in the world, I won't argue with that. But there's also good—everywhere. Focusing on that makes life more enjoyable. So why wouldn't I?" I shrug.

Soren is silent for a moment, considering my words.

"That's... a nice way of looking at it."

I smirk. "You should try it sometime. You might be surprised." I suggest.

He turns toward me, looking slightly offended.

"How do you know I don't already?" he argues.

I snort. "Doesn't take a mind reader to see that you don't."

He scoffs and looks away. I watch him from the corner of my eye, noticing the way the firelight catches his face. *Goddess, he's beautiful.*

"You're good with her." I tell him, thinking of the unexpected softness in his voice earlier.

To my surprise, his cheeks redden. He grumbles, "Thanks."

We lock eyes for a moment, unspoken emotions reflecting to each other. But neither of us acknowledges them.

I don't comment on his physical reaction, giving him a few moments before breaking the silence.

"I'll take the first watch," I say, staring into the fire.

"Okay," he says, his voice tinged with weariness. "Wake me when it's my turn."

I nod, and within minutes, he's asleep.

Hours later, I wake him, and we switch without a word.

As I lie down, exhaustion finally pulls me into a deep slumber.

***

The next morning, we pack up camp and continue heading southeast. Nearly a full day in, we finally reach a creek.

The moment we arrive, I notice the stillness of the forest. No animals. No wind. Just silence. A shiver runs down my spine.

I settle against a large oak tree and wait.

"What are you doing?" Soren asks, his tone laced with annoyance.

"The task said to look in the dark. I'm certain we won't find it before sunset," I state simply.

I pull some bread and water from my pack and hand them to Poderosa. Then, grabbing more for myself, I admire the way the sunlight spills between the trees, casting golden streaks across the forest floor.

By the time we finish eating, all the light has faded. We get up and start looking around.

After just a few minutes of searching, we notice Poderosa has stopped walking. She stares at a cluster of overgrown bushes, her expression unreadable.

Soren and I exchange a glance before moving toward her.

"What is it? Did you find the mark?" I ask, peering over the brush.

"Test." She points at me. "Magic test."

I reach for my magic, but the moment I do, all I feel is frail strings of energy. It has barely recovered since the attack against the eel.

I turn to Soren. "You better get that dirt ready," I joke.

He doesn't laugh. "Can you do this?"

I take a slow, measured breath. "Well, I don't really have a choice."

Stepping forward, I push aside the bushes. A faint green shimmer catches my eye. Embedded in the bark of the tree, about a foot off the ground, is a small amulet, half-covered by the tree itself.

I reach down and touch the amulet. I immediately feel its power. The air shifts, seeming to distort into itself. A greenish glow radiates from the ground below my feet. I faintly hear Soren gasp at the sight, my ears blocked from the change in air pressure.

My vision spins. A surge of magic courses through me, and my eyes roll back as I'm pulled into a magic stamp.

As I look around, I try and remember everything they taught us about magic stamps. It may seem like you are in there for days when it's only been hours in the outside realm. Anything that happens to your spirit body in the magic stamp happens to your real body.

When my senses return, I am no longer in the forest.

I shake off the dizziness and look around. The world around me is old-fashioned—villagers in outdated clothes, dirt roads, vendor stalls.

I glance down at myself and realize I don't fit in.

Rushing behind a nearby building, I sneak past the back of a vendor's cart, snatching an old dress from a pile of fabric. I change quickly, stuffing my own clothes behind a large rock.

As I step back into the clearing, I think to myself, *okay, Adira, focus, you need to find out what the task is to prove yourself.*

I step onto the gravel road, nodding politely at passing vendors.

The scent of fresh bread mixed with the metallic tang of fear fill the air. Faded banners from an old kingdom hang in the street, long forgotten. Just as I near the end of the market, a sudden shift darkens the sky.

The wind picks up.

Smoke rolls in, thick and suffocating.

A figure emerges from the haze—a man in a long, blood-red cloak.

The instant people see him, they drop to their knees, heads bowed.

My heart pounds, but I follow their lead, kneeling while keeping my eyes on him through my lashes.

To my left, an older man hesitates, stealing a glance at the figure.

The man in red sees this and gives a silent nod to one of his guards.

Before I can react, the guard steps forward and cleaves the old man's head clean off.

A muffled sob escapes from the woman beside the now headless man.

My stomach churns, but I force myself to stay still.

The man in red continues forward, his voice booming through the thickened air.

"Where is my offering?"

A woman steps forward, clutching a young child in her arms. Tears stream down her face as she extends the girl toward him.

The man grips the child's cheeks.

I watch in horror as he siphons the magic from her body.

Her skin glows as her power is ripped away, her light dimming until her complexion turns ashen and gray. The child sags in her mother's arms, unconscious. An angry red mark flaws her once pristine skin. The shape of it a vicious wolf. He smirks down at the mark, wiping his fingers together as if brushing off dust.

I bow my head and whisper a quiet prayer for her.

If the history books were right, she will wake in a few hours—alive, but empty. The loss of magic is not fatal, but it leaves something missing. Something that can never be replaced.

A sharp sting slices across my cheek.

I barely suppress a gasp as blood drips from the fresh wound. One of the guards glares down at me, blade in hand. *I must have whispered too loudly.*

Luckily, the man in red is too preoccupied with his prize to notice.

Once he is done, he turns and strolls back to his guards.

"I will return in a fortnight for another offering. Do not disappoint me."

He pauses for a moment, scanning the crowd as if searching for something. I panic slightly, keeping my head bowed. He turns his gaze away, seeming done with his search. With a flick of his fingers, he and his guards vanish into the thick smoke.

The moment they are gone, the tension shatters.

Some women rush to comfort the grieving widow still clutching her husband's headless body. Others surround the mother and her magic-less child, whispering prayers of protection.

The smoke begins to clear, but the damage lingers.

Rising to my feet, I scan the devastation left behind. I take in their worn-out clothes, looking as if they have been patched together over generations, proof of their suffering.

I find a girl standing alone and approach her.

"Hello, I'm Adira. What's your name? Do you know what that was all about?"

She smiles shakily. "My name is Agatha, but I go by Aggie."

She glances toward the retreating smoke before turning back to me.

"That was Diraxsus. He is the most powerful Stregone in existence. He wasn't always this way. He used to be in the same class as me before he got his hands on a book of forbidden spells."

"After his parents died, he... changed. He started stealing magic. First from animals. Then from people. Until no one could stop him."

"Now, every fortnight, he comes to take a child's magic before they reach their eighteenth birthday—before they can fully develop their power."

"Everyone lives in fear of him."

I blink, stunned at the sheer audacity of this man.

I nod firmly.

"Well, that won't do."

Aggie looks at me in shock.

I cross my arms. "We have a fortnight to come up with a plan to stop him."

Looping my arm through hers, I smile.

"Do you have a place where we can talk?"

She hesitates. "Yes... this way."

I catch her skeptical glance and wink.

"Great. Lots to do, then."

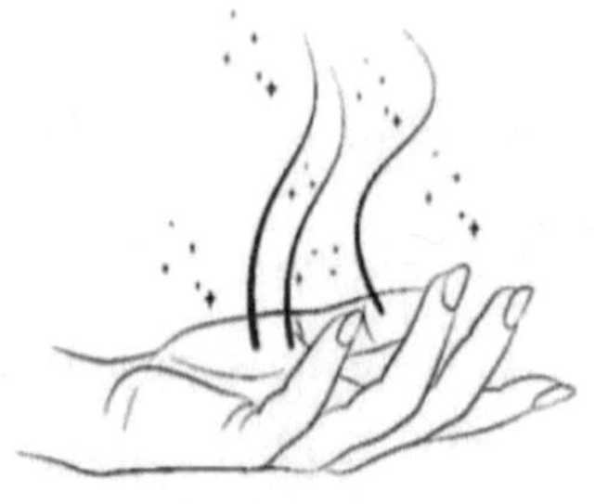

Chapter 13

Once we get to Aggie's house, I settle in at her wooden table as she gets a fire going.

"So, are you fearless or just missing a few screws?" she asks with nervous amusement.

I chuckle. "Neither. I'm just here to save your village."

This must be it. I just need to save the village to prove myself.

I decide not to tell her the whole truth about the magic stamp, just in case it interferes with the goal of proving myself.

She slowly nods. "Okay, then what do you suppose we do? There have been many attempts at killing Diraxsus, but no one has been successful. There's no chance, really, since he put a block on the powers of all the people who live here."

I smile at my in. "And there's the difference. I'm not from here, and I still have my power."

I hold out my hand, palm up, and summon my magic to the surface to show Aggie.

Her amber eyes grow wide. "How is that possible?"

I hear the hope in her voice and grab her hand.

"I will stop him, I promise. I just need your help."

Aggie hesitates a moment, doubt lingering behind her eyes. Her doubt pulls mine to the surface. *What if I'm not strong enough? What if the Vormr has weakened my powers too much?*

Aggie nods excitedly. "Anything."

I straighten my spine at her reply. Summoning up my confidence again.

"That's the response I was hoping for."

***

After some tea, Aggie jumps into a story about Diraxsus' past.

Once he fell off the deep end and started stealing everyone's powers, he could feel the villagers' anger past his cottage walls. He knew he couldn't stay there for his own safety, so he ran off deep into the woods and built himself a large house with the surrounding trees and vines. Still, he felt threatened, so he grabbed the spellbook and found a way to bind everyone's powers. Once that was done, he still needed to ensure the villagers feared him. So, every fortnight, he would come and drain the power of a child before their eighteenth birthday.

Once she finishes, I already have a plan forming in my mind. Since he's using unknown magic, I assume he has an excess power source in his house for backup.

"So, when Diraxsus arrives for the child, I will be hiding in the woods near his house, cloaking myself with magic. Once I feel him leave, I will rush into his house and destroy his excess power source. This will momentarily weaken and distract him. That's where you come in. We'll set a trap to temporarily bind him. All you have to do is trigger the trap. We'll also need some of the villagers to distract the guards while I teleport back and drain the rest of his powers."

Aggie blinks as she absorbs this. "You're going to blow up his power source? And that's just...going to work?" she asks skeptically.

"Yes. I've learned about dark magic users. If he's relying on a power stash, he's more fragile than he wants you to believe."

"And if this doesn't weaken him? What's your backup plan?"

I wave off her concern.

"Trust me. He won't see it coming."

She's silent, seeming to overcome an internal battle.

"If you are certain, I have some men who would happily volunteer to distract the guards."

"That's exactly what I want to hear."

Over the next two weeks, we put the plan into action. We inform the villagers, and many men volunteer to disarm the guards. Aggie leads me into the forest, showing me the quietest and quickest route to Diraxsus' house. The villagers know which part of the forest he lives in, ensuring no one ventures too close.

Once we spot smoke billowing from his house, I tell Aggie to wait there while I sneak closer.

I creep to the edge of the tree line. Taking note of how many guards are milling about. Timing their schedules and routines. I focus on the house, feeling a strange pulsing from the right side.

I walk back to Aggie, satisfied with my findings. We head back to her house and finish preparing for the plan.

Before we know it, the fortnight is upon us. Everyone gets into position in the village, and I head toward Diraxsus' house.

When I see the smoke, I cloak myself in magic and move closer. I stop at the clearing in front of the property. Shortly after, he and his guards step out, and he teleports them to the village. I scan for any magic alarms but find nothing.

I snort. He's gotten overconfident.

I notice his guards have lessened, most going with him to the village. Pausing a moment, I wait for the guard in front to walk around the corner. Once he's out of sight, I slink through the clearing, hurriedly climbing the steps.

I slip inside, following the tug of magic. I push through a wooden door, it creaks slightly, causing me to cringe. Looking behind me, I don't see any guards running toward the sound, so I enter the small room. In the center of the room is a pulsating black orb. Hovering in the air with threads of energy crackling around it. I stay against the walls, as far away from it as I can, not wanting it to sense an unknown power.

I use my magic, setting up an explosive. Placing it beside the pulsing energy, I rush outside, extend my magic, and detonate it. Seconds later, the house explodes, sending up a mushroom-shaped cloud.

I close my eyes, press my hands into the earth, and teleport back to the village.

When I open my eyes, chaos surrounds me. The villagers fight the guards with makeshift weapons. Diraxsus is nearly free from the trap, a half-drained child gasping on the ground beside him. Aggie is yelling at me to hurry.

Diraxsus' voice booms above the noise.

"You think you can defeat me? How many times must you try before you realize I am more powerful than all of you." He shouts out with a mocking tone.

Some of the villagers near him pause in fear, turning and running the opposite way. As if they hope he doesn't remember their faces.

I spring forward. Diraxsus' nostrils flare and his eyes glow with anger, as if he is now realizing I'm the real threat. I smirk as I stalk up to him. *You should be afraid. You should be very afraid.* He thrashes, resisting as I reach for him. Finally, I grasp his face, extending my magic to drain his. It's almost too easy. His head whips side to side, trying to break my hold. Grasping tighter, I will his power into me. He lets out a scream, body contorting in pain. I fight the urge to pull back from him as his veins turn black.

Once I've absorbed the last of it, I release him.

He collapses, glaring at me with pure hatred.

Something feels wrong. Whispers of dark threads fill my head, urging me to commit wicked things. My power intertwines with his. I try to push the corrupted dark magic out, but it latches on, traveling deeper into my reserves. Panic grips me as I stare down at him, struggling against my new dark urges.

"What did you do?" I demand desperately. "What spell can I use to reverse it?"

He laughs bitterly.

Kill him. He deserves to burn. My new internal voice hisses to me.

Before he can answer, a villager steps up behind him with rage in his eyes.

"This is for Esmeralda, you monster. I hope you rot in hell." The villager declares with hatred. He then drags a heavy sword up, slicing Diraxsus' head clean off.

I fall to my knees, defeated. The dark magic is sinking into my soul. I know what I have to do.

Don't do it. The dark voice insists. *Together, we could do remarkable things.*

Gritting my teeth, I ignore the voice. The desire of the tainted power struggling to take control of my will.

I begin reciting the spell I swore I never would—the spell that releases all magic.

"Vires adhibentur, nunc abusi quod olim fovit, nunc dimitti."

Magic drains from my body. The earth swallows up the power eagerly. A hollow emptiness settles in, and tears sting my eyes.

Out of the corner of my vision, I see Aggie running toward me.

"You did it! You saved everyone, Adira!" she exclaims, then notices my expression and halts. "Are you okay?"

I smile weakly as my vision blurs. "Take care of everyone, Aggie."

My thoughts travel back to Soren. *I wonder if he would be proud of me.* Doubt seeps into those thoughts. *No. He needs my power to help him with his blood oath. He won't be happy it's gone.*

Almost like I summoned him, I hear his voice in the distance. Yelling my name. Like a dream calling me.

The last thing I see before I lose consciousness is Aggie's concerned face.

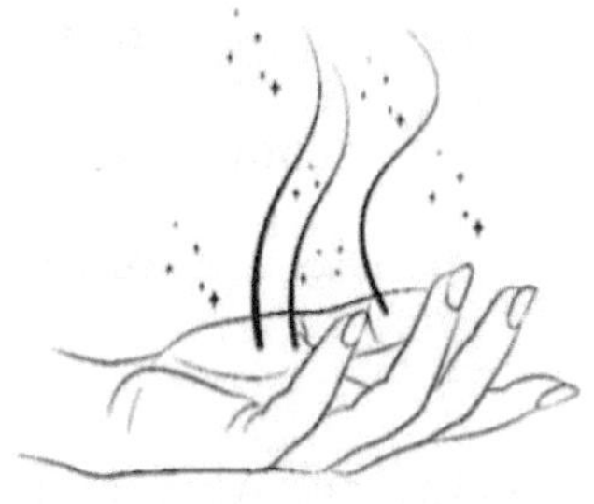

Chapter 14

Once I regain consciousness, I find myself covered in dirt and come face-to-face with Soren and Poderosa. I wrap my arms around myself and feel a tear trickle from my eye as I grimly tell them, "No need for the dirt. My magic is gone."

Soren's body goes rigid, he looks away for a moment, frustration in his eyes.

I sigh heavily at his reaction. *Guess I was right.*

He turns back, taking note of my expression.

Usually it feels better being right.

"I left you alone for one night, and you lost the one thing keeping you alive." Soren jokes, trying to lighten the mood.

"And you." I add bitterly.

He shakes his head.

"Don't worry about me. What happened?" He says sincerely, grasping my hand in his.

"I was gone for a fortnight. Long story short, I was in a magic stamp and needed to release my powers to save the village," I explain sadly.

We find a cave nearby and solemnly turn in for the night, Poderosa and Soren both giving me space as I grieve the part of me that is now gone.

Once Poderosa tucks in for the night, Soren drops down beside me. "Hey, princess," he says softly.

"Hi," I mumble back, too numb to feel anything.

"You'll be fine. I have no doubt. Soon you'll be annoying me again by tripping me with a tree branch."

He gives my arm a squeeze and gets up. A tear leaks out of my eye, and I make no move to wipe it away, letting it clear my vision for my watch.

I stay sitting at the entrance of the cave with my knees drawn to my chest, looking out into the night. I don't know how long it's been, but I hear both Soren and Poderosa softly snoring. My mother's voice breaks into my thoughts, *strength comes from here and here,* she told me, tapping my head and my heart. *And you, my dear, are strong enough to endure anything, I have no doubt.* I dwell on this as the night sky deepens.

Looking toward the stars, I speak to my mother. *I don't know if I'm strong enough for this. I don't know who I am without my power.* I admit to myself, letting the hollow feeling numb me.

A sliver of awareness dances along my spine, and I straighten up and narrow my eyes toward the night.

I see a flash of white to my left and blink away the tears that are still in my eyes. A translucent outline of a woman in a long white dress appears. I shakily get to my feet and head over to her cautiously.

"Eira," I whisper, not feeling any sense of fear.

She grabs my hands. "Adira. You have passed my test. You are worthy of the knowledge."

I watch the line of light that goes through her body and passes into me through our joined hands. My eyes glaze over as I view the true history of Eira and why the mark was hidden. Once the flow of information stops, my eyes clear up, and Eira has vanished. It takes me a moment to notice my powers have returned.

I feel stronger than ever as I grin and glance up at the dark sky, silently thanking Eira. I now understand why the mark was hidden so well: anyone who proved themselves would gain more power than before.

Soon after, the dawn breaks, and they both wake up. I can't contain my excitement as I turn toward them. "My powers are back!" I shout gleefully.

Poderosa claps her hands. "Yay!"

She leaps forward and wraps her arms around me. I meet Soren's eyes above Poderosa's head and give him a wide smile.

"How did this happen?" Soren asks suspiciously.

"Eira came to me in the night. Releasing my powers was her test," I say with a grin. A flicker of admiration enters his eyes. He turns away, attempting to hide it.

I gently unwrap Poderosa from her tight grip around me, setting her down.

I lightly bump my shoulder to Soren's. "Come on, let's eat some breakfast, and I will tell you everything."

We all move deeper into the cave and sit around the small fire we built. I stare into the embers, and my mind wanders back to what I had seen. My grin fades as I start to recount the tale. The lingering bitter feelings from young Eira still remain linked to the current power inside of me.

"It was terrible," I whisper. "She was just a normal, kind young child. They all blamed her for taking their powers. The story doesn't even begin to recount all that she endured: secret lashings, people trying to cut the magic out of her, men forcing themselves on her. She was so strong, and her final act to save the village that treated her so poorly was to sacrifice herself."

I feel my anger rising. "She didn't deserve any of that! She should have let that village burn to the ground."

I stalk out of the cave toward the tree line. My chest grows hot as my magic hums to the surface. I let out a scream of frustration, and a burst of power shoots out of me, causing the trees to explode into flames.

I take ragged breaths as remnants of power pulse in my body. I feel a hand on my arm, and my body jerks at the cool touch. I turn and lock eyes with Soren.

"Take a deep breath, Adira," Soren commands.

I take a deep breath and close my eyes, willing my heart rate to slow. I open them again and look out towards the burning trees. I sink down to the ground and plant my hands in the soil. I push out the element of water mixed with air to douse the trees.

I look out at the charred remains and silently say a quick prayer of apology to the earth.

I turn back toward the fire and notice Soren has returned to Poderosa's side. She's huddled against him as she looks up at me with uncertainty.

A stab of guilt hits me in the chest. I crouch down so that I'm eye level with her. "I'm sorry I scared you, Poderosa," I say as softly as I can. I reach out to comfort her, but she flinches away from my touch. My chest pinches painfully.

She shakes her head at me and curls up closer to Soren.

"I guess this just proves you right about my maternal instincts," I say with a self-conscious chuckle.

Soren clenches his jaw and doesn't laugh. "I didn't m—" he starts.

"Save it," I say bitterly, cutting him off. "I'll pack up the supplies." I glance at Poderosa, still clinging to him.

With a heavy sigh, I start gathering our things. Just as I finish, I spot Poderosa whispering to Soren. He nods, setting her down, and she scampers into the trees.

After a few moments, Soren breaks the silence. "We should talk about the next task—the lost cave of Orlo."

"I've never heard the story," I admit. "Only rumors about the Malgion Mountains."

Soren's lips curl into a secretive smile. "Well, it's a good thing I have, princess."

I raise an eyebrow in disbelief.

He chuckles. "I actually know something about history that you don't. Let me enjoy this moment."

I pause, surprised by the warmth of his laugh. Shaking my head with amusement, I punch his shoulder lightly. "Come on, just tell me."

"There's not much to tell," he begins. "A brave warrior, trying to return home to his love—who was with child—once crossed the rocky overpass of the Malgion Mountains. He had to take the near impossible path to survive in order to protect the truth. A fierce storm forced him to take shelter in a cave. As the wind howled and the cold set in, he realized he wouldn't survive the night. Before his final breath, he wrote down the old King's closely guarded secret—a truth the King would do anything to keep hidden. He sacrificed his life to keep this secret, knowing that he had a family to get to. Though many have searched for the cave, none have found it. The mountains have claimed countless lives—soldiers lost to jagged rocks, snowstorms, and confusion. Some say Orlo himself used magic to conceal the cave and his message."

His face clouds with pain as he talks about Orlo's sacrifice. My mind turns at his reaction, *I wonder what he's had to sacrifice in his life?*

Besides his free will... I answer myself, feeling stupid.

I exhale deeply when he finishes. "That's such a sad story. I can't imagine how his love must have felt."

Soren looks at me, something unreadable in his expression.

"What?" I demand.

He shrugs. "Just an interesting part of the story to focus on."

I brush past his comment. "So, where do we start?"

He surveys the landscape. "Those are the mountain peaks," he says, pointing southeast. Poderosa returns, and Soren wordlessly lifts her into his arms.

"It shouldn't take us long to reach the base," he adds.

"Okay," I reply, turning back toward camp. "Let's get a move on."

"We can't go yet." Soren says, stopping me.

"And why not?"

"For starters, you should rest."

"I'm fine."

He shoots me a look like he doesn't believe me.

"And also, I need to go hunting. We are low on food."

I sigh at his logic.

"Why didn't you do that while I was in the magic stamp?"

"And leave your body unprotected?" He retorts, seeming insulted by the question.

Okay, fair point.

He nods at whatever he sees on my face, turning and walking deeper into the forest.

"I won't be long."

***

When he returns, we gather up our packs and start walking.

Poderosa clings to Soren as we head further south toward the Malgion Mountains. I walk ahead of them, my thoughts consumed by Eira.

I contemplate her and her power. Would I be able to sacrifice my magic and my life? I want to say yes. I need to prove myself to everyone back home. I think about how I left—chased out of my own kingdom, only to be hunted in this one. I glance over at Soren, the ache of having no place to call home settling deep within me. Not after what happened. I squeeze my eyes shut to block out the memory, but it crashes back.

It started as a normal day. I woke up early and headed to the training field, where I saw my friends, Saline and Atin, already sparring. I smiled as Saline brought Atin down to his backside. He shook his head as he stood, rubbing it. I jogged across the field to them, and they greeted me by trying to take me down, two to one. I smirked and dropped into my fighting stance.

Saline went for a quick, straight attack while Atin came at me from the side. I blocked Saline's strike and bent low to swipe at Atin's legs. He bounced back and shot forward again. Twisting Saline and my connected spears, I used the momentum to throw her toward Atin. She stumbled into him, dropping her spear. Seizing the distraction, I knocked his weapon from his hands. They both laughed and raised their hands in defeat.

I stepped back with a grin, wiping a bead of sweat from my forehead. "Nice one," Saline said, her tone impressed. Atin grunted and nodded in agreement.

We trained until our stomachs growled with hunger. As we headed to the dining hall, I broke off. "You guys go ahead. I'll meet you there."

As I turned a corner, I saw the King's mistress, Josephine, speaking with a man known for killing without reason. I stopped short, hiding behind the wall.

"You idiot," Josephine hissed. "You were supposed to kill the King's prized guard stealthily, not slaughter him in front of everyone."

I swallowed a gasp at her treacherous words. The man stuttered, "I apologize, my lady. It was harder than anticipated."

My knees weakened. As I stepped forward to steady myself, my shoe squeaked on the floor. Peeking around the corner, I locked eyes with Josephine. My heart pounded as I turned and stumbled away, abandoning thoughts of the bathroom and dining hall. I rushed back to my room.

Sitting on the edge of my bed, I tried to wrap my head around what I had just witnessed. The only plausible conclusion was that Josephine was plotting to overthrow the King. I stood abruptly and rushed toward the King's sector.

The guards announced me, and I entered the throne room. King Elijah sat with a stony expression. I curtsied and straightened.

"Your Majesty, there is something I must tell you. Josephine is—" I froze as she stepped out from behind a pillar.

"Josephine is what?" she purred, gliding forward, her long blonde hair swaying behind her.

"Enough," King Elijah demanded, his gaze hard.

Her painted red lips curled into a condescending smirk meant only for me before she turned toward the King.

"I apologize, Your Majesty. I'm just so shaken up." Josephine told him with tears in her eyes.

"I understand." The King responded to her before turning to me.

"You dare come in here after what you've done," he said, his voice seething with anger.

My eyes widened, darting between Josephine and the King.

"I—" I began.

The King raised a hand. "I didn't say you could speak. I can't believe you would show your treacherous face after murdering my most prized guard."

The words struck me like a blow.

"I did not murder anyone, Your Majesty. I was framed by Josephine."

She let out a louder sob.

"I can't take these horrid lies."

I resisted the urge to roll my eyes at the dramatic display, instead turning to plead with King Elijah.

"Your Majesty, I have been loyal to you and this kingdom since I came into my powers."

He hesitated for a moment, thinking about my words. Josephine sensed his conflict and struck.

"You must have been planning this for years. Your mother was strange and undisciplined, you must take after her." She insisted.

Understanding dawned on the King's face as he recalled my mother.

"I am nothing like her." I swore to him.

He let out a huff of disbelief and turned to his guards. "Take her to a cell. She will be hanged by morning."

I didn't struggle as they led me away, too stunned to react. As we passed the dining hall, whispers followed me:

'I heard she murdered the King's guard.'

'Her? But she's so small.'

'Wasn't that Saline's brother?'

As if summoned, Saline pushed through the crowd and blocked our path.

"How could you?" she whispered, tears streaming down her face.

I met her eyes, pleading with her. "I didn't murder your brother. I wouldn't do tha—"

Her hand struck my cheek.

"I hope your soul goes to the abyss."

I gasped, staring at my former friend, stunned that she believed the lie so easily.

The guards yanked me forward, dragging me further down the hall. As we passed the large paintings of former rulers, I couldn't help but wonder if I ever belonged here.

The guards took me to the darkest cell.

Halfway through the night, the old scholar, who practically lived in the castle library, sneaked in.

"I'll aid your escape," he whispered, "if you go to Enelon and stop whatever is suppressing the magic in our realm."

Desperate, I took the deal. He handed me a key and vanished into the shadows. I managed to slip away, ignoring the pain of leaving the only place I ever called home behind.

I escaped into the night with only revenge and hope driving me forward.

I shake my head, pulling myself from the memory. Trying to lock it away, into the depths of my mind.

If only it were that easy. But no, I keep feeding on the bitter anger, letting it push me forward.

My thoughts drift back to Eira's story. I compare her choices to my own. Could I really let my realm die? No. *It doesn't matter that they chased me out. It is still my home. The people are still mine.*

I take a deep breath as a renewed sense of purpose floods through me. I will heal our realm. I will clear my name.

I smirk to myself.

Watch out, Josephine.

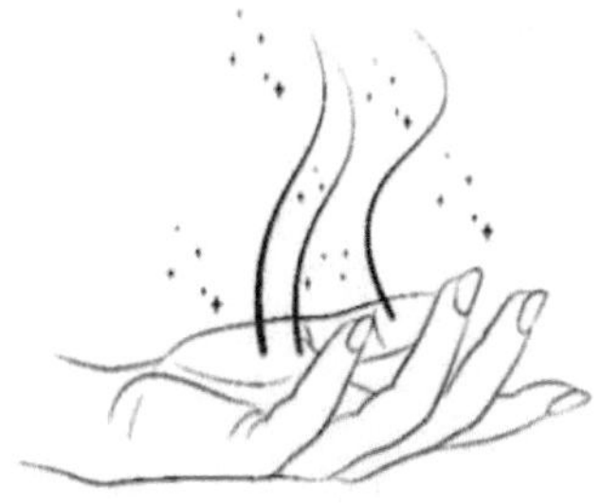

Chapter 15

The next morning, I wake up before dawn. Soren nods toward the edge of the campsite, urging me to follow him. We keep quiet so as not to wake Poderosa.

I glance back at her, and my cheeks heat with shame.

Soren notices. "She'll come around. Just give her time."

I sigh. "I don't blame her. I didn't react in the best way."

"Are you okay now?"

"Yes, I am. Much better." I say, a calmness settling over me.

"Good."

He hesitates for a moment before asking, "After you burned those trees, I noticed a shift in the air. Almost like it was being pulled. Was that you?"

Shit. I didn't even realize I was wielding air.

I look at Soren for a moment, then decide I want to tell him.

"You can't tell anyone what I'm about to share." I speak seriously.

My mind flashes back to the horror stories I've heard about Stregoni with four elements. The rumors about the experiments they would run on them. If only there was a thing more coveted than power in this world.

A shiver travels up my spine.

"I promise," he agrees in a deep voice.

"I mean it. If the wrong person finds out, Soren, I won't just be hunted. I'll be erased."

Concern flickers in his eyes before he masks the emotion. "I understand."

I take a deep breath.

"I can wield all four elements." I admit quickly. It feels like a weight is lifted off my shoulders. *Damn, I didn't know how freeing it would feel to tell someone.*

His jaw clenches and he takes a step away from me.

"Are you serious?"

"Dead serious. And dead I will be, if you tell anyone." I remind him with a pointed look.

He eyes me like he doesn't quite believe me.

"Prove it." He commands with a hard voice.

I hesitate at his tone. My first instinct is to push back on commands coming from a cocky male.

Ignoring the instinct, I focus on the air around me and pull it to the surface. I place my hand palm-up and visualize a small wind tunnel. It whips my hair back. I glance up at Soren's face and see a flash of awe in it. He quickly hides the show of emotion but relief spreads through me. I cut off the magic, and the miniature storm stops, returning the air to normal.

"I thought you'd be angry that I lied." I confess.

He shakes his head as a serious expression covers his face.

"I understand why you did. Sometimes we have no choice but to lie."

I offer him a small smile.

He grabs my hand and gives it a squeeze.

"I know I should be more cautious since you just proved how dangerous you are. But all I can think about is how much trouble you'll be in if someone finds out." He admits softly.

My lips part at his confession.

"I've made it this far. I'll be fine."

"I know you will, princess. For what it's worth, I won't tell anyone. Your secret is safe with me."

I give him a small smile in thanks. Thinking that his words are worth more than he knows.

***

We are passing a small cave when a rumble comes from within. We pause to listen. I slide my dagger out, while Soren does the same with his sword. Poderosa scampers up a tree behind us.

I hear tons of feet moving closer. Seconds later, a group of Hunters comes rushing out.

I swear and grab my sword with my other hand. They stop and look at us, then sprint forward.

I throw a dagger, and it sinks into one of the creature's mouths. I bring my sword up to slice through another one.

Unsure if Soren knows what they are, I yell to him, "Don't let them get too close to you. They'll siphon out your powers."

"I don't have any powers," he reminds me.

I internally roll my eyes and leap back from one of the Hunters.

"What do you call mind-reading?" I point out.

I hear him grunt as he runs his sword across the Hunter's neck.

"Good point," he mumbles.

I notice more swarming out of the cave. *Shit, there are too many.*

One charges me from the side as I feel another step up closer to me. My knees shake as it starts draining my power. The feeling is overwhelming. It's as if I have no control of my magic, it rushes to the surface, bursting through my skin. It travels through a dark funnel of smoke into the Hunter's body.

The sensation cuts off. Its head thumps to the ground. I shoot Soren a grateful look and focus on the Hunter's swarming us. Hope deflates in me at all the creatures.

I see Soren get enveloped in dark bodies, I panic for a moment, but he lets out a primal scream and cuts through them.

Goddess, that was attractive.

The distraction costs me, I don't hear the Hunter coming up behind me until the last second. I turn sharply, wavering as dizziness threatens to take me down.

Before I can lift my sword, it falls to the forest floor, dead. I see an arrow sticking out of its head.

A flash of silver catches my eye from above. I look up just as someone drops down from a tree, right in front of the cave entrance. They start slicing and killing Hunters with skill.

Their hood falls back, and long copper hair spills out. The mysterious girl turns and winks at me with dark blue eyes.

With the three of us, we manage to kill the rest of the Hunters. As I slice the head off the last one, I turn toward the girl.

"Who are you?" I ask warily.

"My name's Esper," she answers brightly.

"What are you doing here? Who do you work for?" Soren interrogates, still holding his sword. He inches closer to me, shielding my body with his.

Esper lifts her hands up in amusement.

"Hey, pal, I'm on your side. Or did you miss seeing me kill all those Hunters to help you?"

I stifle a laugh at her sarcasm.

I don't trust the convenience but without her, I'm not certain we would have won. I watch her expression for any signs of deception.

"Thank you for helping us." I tell her.

"No problem, Adira."

My gaze sharpens on her at my name. Soren tenses beside me, gripping his sword tighter.

"How do you know my name?"

"Oops. Didn't mean to let that slip so early." She admits lightly.

I raise an eyebrow at her, waiting for her to explain.

Soren just gives her a hard look, and she sighs.

"I was sent to help you. But don't ask me by who, because I can't tell you."

"That's suspicious." I say to her.

She sighs heavily. "I know. I don't expect you to trust me, but I am telling the truth. I want to help you."

"How did you find us?" Soren inquires.

She winces, like she knows her answer won't gain her any trust.

"The man who tasked me with helping you told me where you would be."

Okay, he's a male. I file that information away for later.

"How is that possible?"

Esper shrugs. "He had some kind of otherworldly power. That's all I know."

I'm quiet as I think about this. My gut telling me that she isn't a threat.

She looks over at Soren, then back to me.

"A Stregona from Modereo and an assassin from Enelon. How did that happen?"

"It's a long story," I sigh, relenting to my gut feeling. "But right now we're heading to the Malgion Mountains to find the cave of Orlo."

"An adventure... Count me in!" Esper says excitedly.

"No." Soren states.

"Soren, can I talk to you for a moment?" I ask, gesturing to step back to talk.

"Fine. But don't move." He tells Esper.

"Wouldn't dream of it." She replies cheekily.

Soren and I walk away from her for some privacy.

"You can't be serious?" He starts with disbelief. "You want to trust someone we just met. Who just happened to find us?"

"I know it seems irrational, but my gut is telling me to trust her. I didn't sense any deception when she was speaking to us. Plus, we could always use extra help." I finish off.

"This is insane. You know that right?"

I sigh because I do see his point.

"I know it is. But sometimes you need to take a leap of faith. Let this be ours."

"Fine." He reluctantly says. We head back over to Esper.

Soren mumbles something about me being too trustworthy. I ignore him and call to Poderosa. She climbs down the tree.

"This is our travel companion, Poderosa," I introduce to Esper.

She crouches down. "It's nice to meet you, sweetie. I'm Esper."

Poderosa gives her a small smile in return.

Turning to Poderosa I tell her, "Esper will be coming with us to help us on our adventure."

"Okay." She says quietly. I see Esper grin at my statement.

Soren seems to visibly react to Poderosa's innocent voice. He turns to Esper.

"If you betray us in any way, you will wish for death." He promises her with a dark expression.

"Got it." She swallows, visibly shaken by his threat.

I give her an encouraging smile.

"Okay," Soren says. "Let's keep moving."

***

A few hours later, we reach the foothills of the Malgion Mountains. I stare at the steep cliff in front of us and try to think how the hell we are going to scale a mountain.

Soren must know where my head is at because he says, "There is supposed to be a secret pathway."

He says this while his eyes scour over the jagged rocks.

"Are there any clues as to where the path starts?" I ask while walking closer to the mountain.

He sighs and runs his hand through his hair as he tries to remember.

"There was an old saying that to clear the mind from the supposed spell cast by Orlo, one must show trust in one's companions."

I hear my confusion bleed into my voice. "How are we supposed to do that?"

I turn to Esper. "Do you know anything?"

"I was only told the same," she admits.

Soren looks at her mistrustfully before turning to Poderosa.

"Any ideas, Po?"

I smile warmly at his nickname for her.

She points to a smooth portion of the gray stone.

"It's there?" Soren asks.

She nods in response.

"Okay. I trust you." He walks up to the wall poking and pushing it.

"You have to walk through." She says, a sheen of white reflecting in her eyes. Our eyes widen at the display of power.

Doubt flashes across Soren's face but he turns back to the wall.

"Okay. Here goes nothing."

He steps forward and…smashes into the rock.

He curses under his breath as he holds his now bleeding nose.

I bite my lip, trying to hold in my laughter. Glancing over at Esper, I see her doing the same. It bursts out of me, and I double over in laughter. Esper's laughter joins mine. Even Poderosa giggles at the sight.

He grumbles. "It's not funny." But his lips twitch, betraying his amusement.

After our laughing fit ends, we focus back on the task at hand.

Turning to Po, I ask her. "Why didn't that work?"

She has a confused look on her face. "I don't know."

She stares intently at the wall. The white glow sheen flashes over her eyes again.

The confused expression melts off her face, replaced by certainty. She silently walks forward and grabs Soren's and my hands. I grab Esper's with my right. She leads us forward to the wall of gray stone. Soren and I glance at each other over her head with hesitancy.

"Close your eyes," she whispers. I turn to Esper and give her a small nod.

We close our eyes, trusting Poderosa and her gifts.

She takes a few steps forward, and I hold my breath as I wait for my body to slam into the rocky wall. Surprisingly, we keep walking forward, well past where the rocks would have been.

Poderosa stops.

"Open your eyes."

I open my eyes and see we are in a dark cellar. The gray stone around us forms a large circular room. I do a slow turn and notice five crystal balls on pedestals.

Before we can take any more steps forward, the air in front of us flickers. A semi-transparent man with a shaved beard appears. *This must be Orlo*, I think to myself.

"Welcome. If you've made it this far, you have a strong mind. Or some of my magic flowing in you."

We all look at each other with wide eyes and glance down at Poderosa.

"In front of you are five crystal balls, each one showing a thread of what could come from moving forward. You may each look at only *one* crystal ball. If, after, you all agree on moving forward, a path will appear for you, and it will be up to you to brave the treacherous mountain passage. All of your company MUST be in agreement. Otherwise, you will be forced back out and will never be able to return. If you venture forward and lose heart, you may be stuck within my misty realm forever. Once you make your choice, call my name and speak it aloud."

The faded image of Orlo vanishes, and we stay silent for a moment, processing his words.

I clear my throat to break the silence. "Okay, so once we all look through these crystal balls, we need to all be on the same page about moving forward. That doesn't seem so hard."

I feel a trickle of dread in my spine as my mind tells me it won't be that easy.

I glance at Esper. "Last chance to change your mind."

"I'm all in," she responds with a small smile. I can't help but wonder if she gets a choice. *Do any of us get a choice?* I think bitterly. I can't remember the last time I made an important decision regarding my life or actions. It's always been decided for me. First by my mother, then by King Elijah.

Pushing the sickening thoughts out of my head, I do a quick turn of the room and pick a crystal ball at random. My feet move me toward it as my mind runs a million miles a minute, thinking of everything that could go wrong. I internally shudder as I reach the white sphere.

The shimmering crystal ball stands on an ornate base made of carved wood. I take in the carvings and notice they are people, mid-scream, reaching out to nothing. I swallow my fear and look to my companions.

I notice the others have also chosen one. We all look at each other and nod.

Soren locks eyes with me. "See you on the other side," he says with forced lightness.

I attempt a smirk and turn back to my crystal ball.

I swallow against my dry throat and lean in close, reaching my hands out to grip both sides of the ball. The air whips through the room, turning denser as a light blue tint fills the space.

I feel my eyes roll back from the pressure as I am thrust into a vision almost as vivid as a magic stamp.

It's us as we are now, in the room with the crystal balls. There is a door that has appeared for us behind one of the pedestals. We all walk through it and come out on the outside of the mountain on a newly shown path.

After the slow start, the vision begins jumping to moments.

The four of us shivering around a fire. I feel the coldness seeping into my bones from the unusual weather. I hold Poderosa's small fingers, she's so cold they are almost blue.

A man with a large knife coming toward Poderosa, she screams in fright. Soren jumps in front of her. He takes the knife to the stomach. My own breath stops as he falls to the ground.

Me hanging off the edge of a cliff, while Esper falls to the shallow, rocky water below. A sob rips through me at the sight. My hand begins to slip. As I fall, my thoughts filter through images of my life. Before I make it to my fourteenth birthday, I slam into the ground. Darkness envelopes me, obscuring the pain.

All of a sudden, my eyes snap back to the front of my head, and I fall to the ground in the cave. My chest aches from the visions and the feeling of dying.

I blink away the remnants of the vision, shaking my head in horror as my mind replays the images.

I turn and see the others coming out of their vision haze.

Soren takes one look at me and says, "No. Absolutely not."

My eyebrows raise at his declaration.

"What exactly did you see?" I ask curiously.

Before he can answer, Poderosa leaps into his arms and hugs him tight. She is shaking with tears.

"It's okay," he says soothingly. "None of that happened."

I lock eyes with him and see that his voice says one thing, but his eyes have a slightly alarmed look in them.

I glance down at Poderosa. "Do you want to tell us what you saw?"

She sniffles but lifts her head up from Soren's neck.

Staring straight into my eyes, she says, "I saw you die."

Chapter 16

I blink back the shock of what she just told me. Soren's eyes widen slightly, and his tan skin pales. He hugs Poderosa close to him again and says to me, "We can't go forward. I saw you die too."

I feel the blood drain from my face as I think about my vision.

"I may have also seen my death." I admit quietly. Soren freezes with my admission.

"Then it's decided. It's not happening." He states with agitation.

"Well, that's just three out of the five possibilities. We don't have much of a choice," I say weakly, though uncertainty seizes me. *Will I die?* I push that thought out quickly. Worrying won't help.

"Plus," I add guiltily, "in my vision, I also saw you die, Soren, and Esper."

They both pause, silent as they think about that potential outcome.

Soren scowls. "Great, so it's almost inevitable that someone dies."

I glance back toward the unseen crystal ball.

"That's not true. We could all come out on the other side."

We all fall silent. No doubt weighing the outcomes and our chances.

Esper pipes up, breaking the silence, "I didn't see you die, Adira." Soren ignores her and pleads with me with his eyes.

"Well, we need to all be on the same page about moving forward, and I won't be. So, there." He says with a definite tone.

My frustration turns to anger.

"I don't know what your problem is!" I shout.

"Even if I do die, you can just go back to your lives. Since it seems that I'm the most likely to die," I force out. "I should get to choose. And I choose going forward." Fear grips me as I power through the words. *Fate can be changed.* I remind myself. *We just need to be extra careful. That should be easier now that we know the potential deadly areas.* I tell myself this, even though I know it won't be that easy.

Soren's jaw is clenched so tight I'm surprised it doesn't break. He seems to be having an internal struggle with himself.

I sigh and soften my tone, knowing that if either of them died, I would have a hard time just 'going back to my life'.

"Listen, Soren, we need to go forward. This is about more than us. Think about your realm and mine. Think about Poderosa."

He looks away with a scowl.

I put my hand on his arm. He glances down at me.

"This needs to be done," I say softly but firmly, trying not to let myself read into his sudden protectiveness.

"I just don't want to see you get hurt, princess." Soren admits quietly to me.

My chest flutters at his confession. I open my mouth, then shut it. Momentarily at a loss for words.

"If we don't do this, my magic will be drained, my home destroyed. That is guaranteed pain. At least with this situation, we could all come out on the other side alive. We could stop the Vormr in Modereo and you can get out of your blood oath. At least with this, there is hope."

He gives a resigned nod, I breathe out a shaky breath, glad that my false bravery worked.

Soren eyes me a moment longer, as if he can see through me. The look in his eyes tells me that he won't let me die. I want to believe it.

Then, he looks down at Poderosa.

"What do you say, Po? Are you up for another adventure?"

Poderosa nods with open eyes. "We have to keep going."

Her woeful tone makes her sound older than her years.

I turn to Esper, who has gone quiet.

"I'm sorry you got yourself stuck with us."

She shoots me a light smile. The contrast of the action vastly different from the somber mood.

"I came here to help you. Just because it's gotten more complicated doesn't mean I am going to bail. Plus, I only died in one of the visions, so my odds aren't the worst." She declares.

I smile at her optimism.

"We are lucky to have you with us then."

She smiles warmly back. "I feel lucky to be here and to be a part of your story."

Soren gives her a nod of approval at her words. *That's as nice as it'll get with him,* I imagine.

"Okay, ready?" I ask them all. They nod back.

"Orlo." I speak his name aloud. "We will venture forward as one."

Suddenly, the temperature increases, making the air seem thick and muggy. A light breeze sweeps through the cave, traveling into one of the walls. The wall releases a cracking sound, small fissures appearing in the stone. Then, the rocks fall into themselves, and a doorway is revealed.

"I have to admit, that was pretty neat," I voice.

Soren and Esper chuckle lightly.

"Let's rest here for the night before we move on," I say while glancing at the door.

"Good idea," Soren agrees as he starts to unroll the bedding.

We don't say much to each other as a grim silence stretches around us, all of us lost in our own thoughts of what is to come. I notice Soren watching me as I set up my bedding, an intense look in his gaze. Esper looks nervous as she helps Poderosa with hers. Poderosa clings to her, still seeming frightened by the visions.

Before we fall asleep, I catch Esper up on the journey so far. Her eyes widen with each obstacle we had to pass. After I finish our tale, she sits silently for a moment, as if lost in her own memories.

Turning to me, she hesitates before she speaks.

"I lost my parents when I was young. They were trying to help me escape Modereo."

"Escape Modereo? Why?" I ask, shocked that I wasn't aware she was from there.

She pauses.

"I was different. Society wasn't ready to accept me." Esper says cryptically.

I sense her indecision. "Whatever it is, you can tell me. I wouldn't ever do anything to put you in danger."

A troubled look flashes across Soren's face, so fast that I almost miss it. But he nods in agreement.

Taking a deep breath, she holds her hand out. A mixture of power bursts out, swirling together. The air crackles in response to the new energy.

"I can wield four elements."

I let out a little gasp.

"When the King found out, he tried to capture me. My parents managed to sneak me away, and we went through a natural portal. We ran into some guards, and my parents distracted them as I ran. I heard their screams moments later. I found a small village that took me in. I lied about my powers. Since magic is more muted in this world, I didn't need to worry about any big outbursts that would alert anyone. But I was always afraid I would be found. So, every year, I would pack up and move to a new village. It's exhausting starting over, again and again, but at least I'm alive."

"I'm so sorry, Esper. What you've had to endure? I can't imagine how difficult it must have been. I also know what it's like having no parents," I say solemnly, attempting to ease her loneliness.

"Just know you aren't alone," I tell her and summon my own power up for her to see.

"Y—you can wield all the elements too?"

Confusion and hope mixing in her expression.

I smile. "Yes, I can. I've been hiding it since I was sixteen. It is difficult to hide, but I've managed to build a life in one place with it. You can too. Maybe after this is done, you can come back with me to Modereo. We can figure something out."

Uncertainty flashes across her face.

"If we can figure out a way that ensures I'm safe, then yes, I would love to. I miss that realm so much." She admits wistfully.

Grabbing her hand, I squeeze it in comfort.

"Then let's find a way to make sure it happens." I promise her.

She smiles in response, her eyes glistening with unshed tears.

Soren stays silent as Esper and I talk late into the night about our magic and Modereo.

Eventually, we all fade off, the lingering protection of Orlo filling the room.

***

I wake first, stretching my arms above my head and feeling in a better mood after the previous night. The others wake shortly after, to the sound of me rolling up my bedding.

I look at them. "Are you ready for this?"

Soren takes a deep breath and answers first. "As ready as I'll ever be."

Esper gives a quick nod.

"That'll have to do. Let's get moving." I say, slinging my bag over my shoulder.

Before I take another step, Poderosa runs up to me and hugs my legs. I crouch down to her. "What's wrong?"

"Will you keep me safe?" She asks, vulnerability shining in her eyes. My heart clenches at the sight.

"I will do everything in my power to keep you safe, Poderosa." I promise her, giving her a squeeze back.

Her scared expression lessens. I give her what I hope is a reassuring smile. Soren catches my eye, communicating to me that no matter what, he will also keep her safe.

I shoot him a small smile in thanks, noticing the tension from yesterday's conversation still lingering between us.

We all step through the archway of the gray stone door.

We are met with dark, rolling hills that span out for miles. Thunderclouds fill the sky, and the wind whips the trees from side to side. The atmosphere feels unnatural, the air tugging slightly at my magic.

In the distance, we see a large mountain with the winding path that we must take.

Unease trickles into me as I feel some of my magic depleting. I've barely been feeling it getting lower, with my mind being distracted, but I've noticed it's taking longer and longer to heal. Hopefully, we can make it through all these tasks before it disappears completely. I quickly swallow that fear and trudge forward.

Based on the distance to the mountain, it looks like a four-day walk.

The first day passes without any issues. Esper and Poderosa walk ahead of us, with Esper creating fun air creatures to entertain Poderosa.

Soren watches them, a light expression on his face. A vast difference from the hostile look he usually gives Esper.

"You have to admit, Esper's great," I tell Soren, bumping his shoulder with mine. He draws his attention to me, the mistrust bleeding back into his face.

"I don't trust her. It was all too convenient. Plus, I can't read her mind."

"You remember when I was telling you to look on the bright side of things more often? This is one of those times," I respond cheekily.

His lips threaten to twitch up, but he keeps a straight face as he sighs. "Okay, I'll give it my best shot."

"That's all I'm asking for." I smirk back.

His fingers brush against mine as he turns his attention back to the path. A tingle of awareness goes through me from the light touch.

A blush reddens my cheeks. *I really hope my visions don't come true,* I think to myself, glancing at him from the corner of my eye.

His attention doesn't waver, but I catch a half-smile flicker on his face from my gaze.

We walk the rest of the day in companionable silence.

***

The second day starts off like the first, but then the air changes. The wind picks up, turning the air colder. The clouds take on a light gray hue. We bundle tighter into our clothes and keep trudging along. The violent wind whips us around, pushing at Poderosa's tiny body. We form a small circle around her, trying to block the harsh weather.

Then, the clouds turn an even deeper gray, and they let loose a torrential downpour. Our clothes are soaked in seconds.

We walk through the heavy rain until nightfall, all of us shivering with each step. The mud slick beneath our feet, making each step feel slippery.

Esper holds a hand out, motioning us to stop.

"Something is different about this rain." She shivers out.

"You're right. It's not replenishing my magic," I acknowledge.

As we stand there, we shake our legs out. Mine feel tense from the cold weather. Looking ahead, I notice the rain pooling onto the path, rising quickly. Soren notices the same thing.

"We need to stop for the night. That path ahead will be completely covered by the time we reach it. Plus, it will make things harder if we catch an infection."

"I a-agree," I say through chattering teeth. Soren doesn't look toward me at my agreement, his body wrought with tension. *Is it from the weather? Or is he still upset about yesterday?* Esper's voice drags me from my spiraling thoughts.

"Me too," Esper shivers out.

We find a semi-dry spot under a large oak tree and set up our bedding.

Soren comes back with some damp wood and looks to me. I summon my magic to dry the logs and send a spark of heat into them.

After a second, they roar to life, heating the area. We all move closer to the fire and spread out our hands.

A sense of dread fills me as my mind flashes back to the vision the crystal ball gave me—a vision of the four of us sitting around the fire, shivering. *What can I do to ensure the other visions don't come true? Perhaps, I should tell the others, then we can look out for any threats.*

I decide that I should keep quiet for now, so I don't worry them. But I vow to myself to be more attentive and cautious moving forward.

I'm not sure I could live with myself if the others got hurt because I forced them into this.

Swallowing hard, I clear my throat. "We need to take our clothes off to dry them."

"You're right," Soren agrees.

He turns around while I help Poderosa and get her settled into her bedding.

"Can Esper sleep beside me?" Poderosa asks shyly.

I turn to Esper in question.

"Of course I can," Esper tells Poderosa, settling down next to her.

We set Poderosa up as close to the fire as we can. Esper lays down on the other side of her. They whisper quietly to each other for a while. Then, Poderosa turns her face towards the fire, and as her face gets some color back, she fades off to sleep. Esper dozes off shortly after.

Soren wanders over to the other side of the fire to change. As his back is turned, I quickly strip out of my dripping clothes and jump into the bedding.

I turn back towards the fire and catch a glimpse of his toned back through the flames. He starts to turn, and I whip my head to the side, cheeks flaming from almost being caught.

I hear him clear his throat, and I turn towards him. He is standing beside me, covering his lower half with his bedding. I feel my gaze linger on his abs as my eyes move towards his face.

He's looking down at me with a heated stare. "My bedding is wet from the rain. Do you mind if we share?"

Do I mind? Um, yes, it most definitely is not a good idea.

My brain screams at me, but I say, "Sure," and lift a corner up for him.

He slides in, and I immediately feel my body temperature rise.

He turns so we are face to face. The fire crackles loudly around us. Since yesterday, the tension between us has increased. I just don't know if it will shatter into anger or lust.

The silence stretches. His eyes briefly flicker to my lips, I find my own gaze mimicking his. Thinking we should talk about the horrifying visions, I drag my gaze up. Hesitating when I see his blue eyes piercing into me.

"Hi," he whispers.

His eyes swirl with emotion.

"Hi."

"I was thinking, when this is all over, you can come see what my realm is all about," I say, trying to keep the vulnerability out of my voice.

"I like that idea, princess." He pauses. "And I like you."

My eyes go wide.

He has a small smile on his face at my reaction.

I huff out a laugh of disbelief. "Well, shit. I happen to like you too."

"Don't sound too pleased about it," he grumbles out, amusement dancing in his eyes.

"We know nothing will come of it," I remind him, giving him a pointed look. His jaw tightens at that.

I can't handle the intensity in his eyes, so I turn on my back.

"Once we are done, we'll go our separate ways and will likely never see each other again."

"I know, Adira. It doesn't change how I feel now," he states with a sigh.

My heart gives a little jump with the comment, and I press my hand to my chest. Affection flaring up.

I think about my visions coming true and the sequence of what will happen, and I lose all thought. *Who cares if this complicates things? I may not live through this.*

Turning back on my side, I move the remaining distance between us and seal my lips on his.

He grunts in surprise but recovers fast. I feel his hand sliding around my hip to my back. He tugs me closer so I'm chest-to-chest with him. I gasp at the extra contact.

As he deepens the kiss, my body tingles in all the right places.

We both pull back, breathing heavily, and look towards the others, seeming to remember we aren't alone.

I look back to him and find his stare already on me. He hesitates a moment, then places a light kiss on my lips. I feel myself soften at the intimate gesture. A look of something flashes across his face. Guilt? Uncertainty? Before I can ask, he shakes it away and pulls me against him.

I let myself forget about what he could be conflicted about, choosing to be content in the moment.

The heat of the fire and his body lull me into sleep.

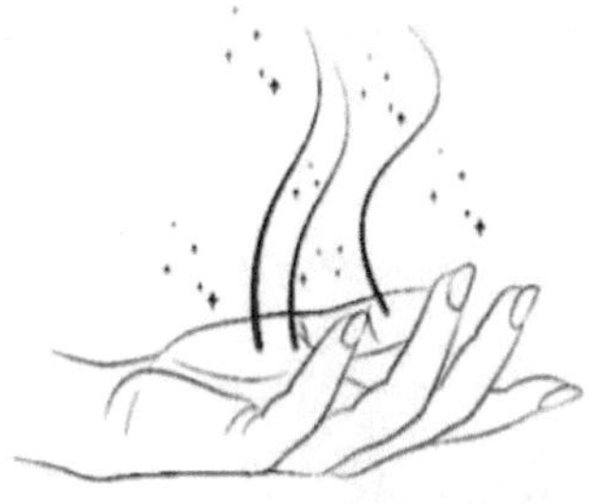

Chapter 17

A sharp snap echoes through the forest, jolting me awake. My heart pounds as I scan the darkened surroundings, searching for what disturbed the silence. I detect wildlife moving deeper in the forest and relax slightly. Glancing up, I see that the dark storm clouds have vanished, leaving only light, cream-colored ones scattered across the sky. The wind, though still whipping, has softened since the rainstorm.

I glance down at Soren's sleeping form, a small smile tugging at my lips. Slipping into my now-dry clothes, I stand on the damp leaves. Poderosa stirs, then approaches me with a shy expression. I open my arms wordlessly, and she leaps into them. I squeeze her tight before letting her go, relieved that she no longer seems uneasy around me.

Feeling lighter than I have in days, I pack our gear, leaving only the food. As Esper and Soren wake, we share a quick breakfast before resuming our journey through the rolling green hills. As the day passes, an eerie stillness settles in the air. My eyes dart through the forest uneasily. I swear I see flickers of shadows scampering between the trees, but when I blink, they are gone. I try to tamp down my apprehension, but the nagging sense of dread creeps over me and lingers throughout the rest of the morning.

By mid-afternoon, I understand why.

Distant voices reach our ears. We move swiftly, taking cover behind a cluster of trees. I stretch out my magic and detect five figures. Peering ahead, we spot a campsite—five large, rugged mountain men stroll around, their supplies suggesting they've been here for some time.

"I think we should go around them," I whisper to Soren and Esper.

They nod in agreement, and we slip deeper into the forest, aiming to give the group a wide berth. Each step we take is taken with caution. We move as silently as wraiths, making no noise.

A twig snaps to our left. We freeze in place but hear nothing else. After a minute of listening, we start forward again. Footsteps thundering through the trees sounds to our right. We all turn toward it, arming ourselves.

Suddenly, someone crashes through the bushes behind us. A spark of energy hits us, knocking us to the ground. The impact is swift. Darkness presses in, and as my eyes flutter closed, one panic-ridden thought lingers: *How did I miss sensing them?*

***

The acrid smell of burning wood wafts in the air, waking me. Opening my eyes, I see that we are bound by invisible restraints. Before

I reach for my magic, I look up and see six angry-looking male faces. The one I had missed before looks at me with sharp eyes.

I hold in a gasp as I realize why I didn't sense him before. My heart spikes with fear as I feel his magic pulsing below the surface of his skin. I pull against the bindings trapping my hands, feeling momentarily powerless.

"Who are you?" I direct at the sixth person. He tilts his head. "Who are you?" He pauses, leaning in uncomfortably close. "You are like me." Then he pulls back, tilting his head toward Esper. "As are you." The others look between him and us at that statement. He watches us with an unsettling stillness, his eyes unblinking. I suppress a shiver at the intense look.

I force my attention away, focusing on the other men. I try not to squirm beneath their leering gazes. "Who are you guys, and what are you doing here?" the larger man gruffly says. Internally, I roll my eyes, *I'm so sick of men demanding things.*

I clear my throat. "Same as you, I imagine."

He sneers at my tone. "You don't even know what you've done. You will be trapped in here forever. It's impossible to leave."

A hopeless look flashes across his face. His face hardens again as he turns his attention back to us.

"You're all full of hope and confidence." He says and they all laugh bitterly.

The big man leans in closer, "well, guess what? So were we."

Soren swallows visibly.

"How long have you been here?"

"We've been here for seven years."

My eyes widen at that. Doubt sinking in as I think about our odds. I notice Esper's shocked expression.

The big man eyes us.

"But who knows? Maybe you will be our way out." His tone doubtful.

"That's if we agree to help you."

Soren jumps in at my response.

"What she means to say, is what would we get in return for helping you?" He reasons, shooting me a 'be silent' look.

I notice Esper sizing up the men, searching for weaknesses.

"You would get to live." One of the men respond flatly.

Esper decides to pull out her sarcasm. "Woah. Way to uncomplicate it. So, if we help you, we live. But, if we refuse to help you, you'll kill us?"

Some of the men laugh.

"Exactly, you've figured it out."

She pretends to think about it. "What about a third option? I don't like the current ones."

Soren sighs exasperatedly.

A giggle escapes me, the large man whips his head at the sound, slapping me across the face with the back of his hand.

"Shut up, witch," he sneers. "You are our captives, so, you will do as we say."

A flash of fear crosses Soren's face. It quickly melts into anger.

"Don't. Touch. Her." Soren growls darkly as he struggles against his bindings. The larger man turns his attention to Soren, and I feel my stomach dip at the look of hatred in his eyes. Soren holds his head firm and doesn't break eye contact. The larger man cocks his fist back and drives it into Soren's stomach.

He grunts, and I wince as though I feel it too.

After he takes a few more hits, my anger brings my magic to the surface. I hesitate, wondering how much I want to reveal about myself and my powers. But as the man rears back his leg to kick Soren, I curse to myself. *To hell with the consequences.* Taking a deep breath, I release my power at the men, and they all get blown back. After my quick release of magic, my wrists snap together as the invisible restraint is put back in place. Esper has a slightly shocked look on her face, as if she can't believe I was able to wield while binded.

The Stregone with the slicked-back hair is grinning wide at me. I feel my skin crawl as he walks forward and doesn't break eye contact.

Unwelcome energy prods at me, making my skin prickle uncomfortably at the feeling. I shield myself from his inquisitive power. His eyebrows raise slightly when he can't sense anything. An intrigued look crosses his face. The rest of the men are yelling in anger as they stumble to their feet.

"Keln, what's going on inside their heads?" the smallest man asks in an even-tempered tone.

I look back up at the creepy man, Keln, and see him start to call his magic to the surface. I quickly shut my eyes and call upon my own magic to make a barrier in my mind and Soren's. Poderosa's and Esper's minds still feel impenetrable when I push my own magic against theirs to test it. Esper gives me a nod when she feels my magic, signaling she's prepared.

I notice Soren's calculated gaze scan the area, he shifts to his right, trying to move closer to me. I almost smile at the attempt, but the urgency of the situation takes control.

Shifting my gaze right, I notice Poderosa is still unconscious from when they knocked us out. I try not to panic and focus on my magic. I feel Soren turn his gaze on me, but I keep my eyes shut in concentration.

Keln grunts in frustration, and I feel the pressure ease off. I open my eyes and see him crouched down in front of me. I avoid the need to recoil and look him right back in the eyes. A disturbed look fills his face, like he can't believe he failed.

"My, my, someone is strong," he says with that creepy head tilt of his. He leans in even closer, the crease between his brows deepening. "How did you manage that?" He half-whispers.

Before I can answer, he looks behind him and says, "Hock. Grab them and tie them to the trees over there."

The larger man, now known as Hock, comes up and grabs us one by one, tying us to the trees just on the edge of the clearing. Keln watches the whole time and tasks the small man, Lief, with watching us.

"Especially watch the witches. We don't want them to pull any tricks," he says while he pulls out a small silver chain. "This chain will suppress magic."

My heartbeat picks up at the sight of the chain.

"Which one should I put it on?"

Keln looks between Esper and me. He nods his head toward me. "Put it on her," he decides.

I involuntarily hiss as Lief brings the chain closer to me. I sense Soren looking over at me in concern.

Lief snaps the chain on me, and I immediately feel myself weaken. The burning sensation runs up my arms from where the chains touch my exposed skin. They don't bother tying me to a tree because the chains sap any strength I have.

I squeeze my eyes shut in agony, refusing to show these men how much pain I'm in.

Once I feel I have a grasp on the pain, I open my eyes. I force a smirk to my face when I see all the men watching me.

They scoff and go over to the fire, while Lief sits on a stump facing us. The forest behind us eerily quiet as we sit captive.

"Are you alright, Adira?" Esper asks quietly from my left, the question seems to echo in the silence.

I turn my head toward them, gritting my teeth at the effort. Soren's hands clench at the question, waiting for my response.

"It's a Makutu chain. It goes against my magic, and since my magic is me, it rejects my body," I say through thin breaths. "My magic is recoiling in pain and the longer these stay on me, I will start losing time." Soren looks confused.

"It will cause lapses in my memory. So, I've been better." I wince out. His body tenses at the sight of my wince.

His worried eyes don't leave mine.

"What can I do?" he asks.

"We need to get out of here. Fast."

Esper leans closer to us.

"Keln's charmed my ties, my magic is trapped. But I'm working on breaking the spell." She tells us, her face twisted in concentration.

Movement draws my attention. Soren is shifting discreetly from side to side.

"What are you doing?" I ask him.

"There's a sharp piece of bark behind me. I'm trying to fray the rope." He whispers.

I feel hopeless as I watch them work. I mentally read through the history book about magical suppressants, trying to recall anything about the Makutu chain. A wave of dizziness passes through me, drawing my attention away from my task. One panicked thought remains, screaming louder than the rest.

Get. Them. Off.

Chapter 18

As night falls, the fire crackles, casting flickering shadows across the men's faces. Laughter turns harsh, slurred words mixing with the scent of alcohol. Their excited voices carry over to us. They talk of escape, and my stomach knots. The malicious tone revealing that our escape won't be so easy. *They speak as if they will do anything to get out of here. Including sacrificing us for whatever they need to do.* A shudder rolls through my body. I try to think of a plan, but my head turns foggy, emptying all my thoughts out.

Letting my head fall back against the tree, I glance at our captor. I thought they would switch watch, but it seems Keln doesn't trust anyone the way he trusts Lief.

"Poderosa," I whisper to her still form. "Wake up, honey." I try not to let panic take over.

I glance to my left, hoping one of them is free, since these chains are sapping all my strength. I lock eyes with Esper. She gives a short nod and glances down at her hands. I follow her gaze and see that her hands are free. She whispers a spell with her freed power, and Soren's chains break apart. Sweat beads her brow from the exertion of unraveling the charm. Noticing the signs of mental exhaustion, I shoot her a look. Trying to convey to her that she should conserve her magic.

Turning my attention ahead, I notice most of the men have either passed out or disappeared into their tents. I keep a neutral expression as I think of a plan to distract Lief.

"Hey," I say, my voice croaking. Lief turns his gaze on me.

"What?" he barks.

To my right, I hear a slight stirring, and relief grips me as Poderosa wakes up.

I focus on Lief and push as much strength into my voice as I can. "I think the chains are failing. Would be a shame if I got my magic back," I tell him, forcing a smile.

A flash of panic briefly crosses his face, but he quickly schools his features. I latch onto that panic. I wiggle my body and close my eyes, disregarding the wave of pain the movement brings me.

"Ah, finally," I say convincingly.

I open my eyes and notice Lief is standing. He strides closer to me, eyeing me intently. I maintain eye contact, ignoring that my body is screaming at me to collapse to the ground. A harsh unnatural wind whips through the clearing.

Thank you, Esper.

I smirk with confidence. He visibly pales, no doubt thinking the display was from me.

He fixes us with a glare. "Don't move." He turns and quickly heads toward Keln's tent.

My head snaps to Esper. "Hurry. Get Poderosa's chains off."

Esper closes her eyes and whispers the same spell. Nothing happens. Twisting toward her, I notice her slumped against the tree.

Digging her hands into the soil, she tries again. This time they come off. She gets shakingly to her feet, swaying slightly.

Soren jumps up, helping me stand. Esper grabs Poderosa by the hand, and we turn, taking off deeper into the forest.

A few minutes later, we hear the men shouting, searching for us.

I turn to Esper. "Do you have enough strength to hide us from Keln?"

She hesitates.

"No need." A slick voice says.

I gasp as Keln strolls into view. He gives us a wicked smile at our shock.

"You didn't believe it would be that easy, did you?"

We stay silent.

"You did?" He laughs meanly.

"Considering one of you is a prisoner to the Makutu chain and the other can barely stand? I like my chances." He states confidently.

He holds his hand out, a wave of water shoots up through the damp soil. It bends into a curved beast with two heads. Slithering forward like a snake, it releases a beam of water at us, turning to ice in the air. We dodge the blast, it impales a tree behind us.

Determination sweeps across Esper's face. My pulse stutters at the sight. *She's going to burn herself out.* I think grimly.

As Keln readies another blast, Poderosa steps forward. Her eyes blazing white. He pauses, staring at the child.

She waves her hand lightly through the air. The water beast dissipates easily. Keln's mouth drops open in shock. She has an angry look on her face as she stares him down. She raises her hand again. The ground below Keln opens up, he falls through before he can even react. Glancing down, I can't see an end in sight.

The hole snaps shut.

Poderosa's eyes return to normal. Silence descends on our group. *Holy goddess, I have never seen that level of power before. Not in any realm. Where did she even send him?*

A jolt of apprehension goes through me at the display of power, but I push it aside, noticing her unsettled expression. Esper reaches her first.

"Hey, don't worry, Poderosa. You just saved us." Esper tells her softly.

Poderosa nods back, her troubled look lessening.

"Where did you send him?" I ask, my voice scratchy.

She shrugs. "I don't know. I just wanted the bad man gone."

A shiver runs through me at her response. *Who knows where he will end up? Maybe hell?*

Soren stares at her, his mouth slightly agape. I nudge him, drawing his attention away. He shakes it off and gives her a small smile.

The men's voices start shouting again, getting louder as they unknowingly close the distance.

I sway slightly, the adrenaline wearing off. Soren swoops me up into his arms. I open my mouth to argue that I'm fine, but he cuts me off.

"For once, princess, just let me take care of you." He murmurs softly.

I sigh wearily, trying to push through my fatigue. My body sags against him with relief while my mind calls me helpless and weak. Relenting, I nod. The men sounding alarmingly close.

We start running, trying to put as much distance as possible between us and them.

I jostle in Soren's arms, the motion causing me to black out for a moment. When I come to, the pain is dulling my senses. My body no longer feels like my own. My limbs feel heavy, hanging limply in Soren's arms. Dead weight. The sensation of warmth against my frozen skin coaxes me into oblivion.

***

When I come to, I blearily see that we are behind a wall of vines. I groggily blink my eyes open further and try to move. A clanging noise fills my ears, and I look down at my still-chained hands.

I shiver with pain and notice my head is on Soren's leg. I feel him shift, and I look up at him, a cold sweat covers my body from the movement.

"How are you feeling?" he asks in a quiet voice.

I notice Poderosa sleeping to the left of us.

"Weak," I admit. "I need to get these chains off."

"You've been out for a full day. Esper tried to get the chains off, but she wasn't able to. I couldn't find anything around here to try to take those off you either," he says apologetically.

I hear Esper's voice and turn toward it.

"I'm sorry, Adira. I know those chains are said to be unbreakable, but I tried."

"It's okay. I know it's impossible unless the one who put them on takes them off."

"There must be another way," Esper states.

I hum in agreement and start to shift my weight. Soren helps me sit up, and we hear Poderosa stirring.

She walks over to us. "You're hurt," she accuses quietly.

I smile weakly. "How are you?" I ask Poderosa with concern, recalling her show of power. "Are you tired?"

"I'm fine," she says, shaking her head. Awe fills me at the ease of her magic. *She doesn't seem drained in the slightest.*

"I can help you." She tells me quietly. Emotions flitter through me, disbelief overpowering the rest.

"Can I?" She asks, eyes downcast as if I'll say no.

"That would be incredible. Thank you, Po. And about what happened earlier..."

She nervously shuffles her feet at my words.

"We are glad that you saved us. Don't even think about it anymore."

Esper frowns at that last part, not seeming to agree with my 'shove feelings down' method.

Poderosa smiles hesitantly, relaxing slightly.

She takes another step toward me, and I feel her little hand on my arm. She closes her eyes, and her skin fills with a soft, white glow. My eyes widen as I watch her, mesmerized.

A second later, the chains fall to the ground with a soft clunk. I look down at them, then back up to Poderosa. She looks at us shyly.

"How did you do that, Po?" Soren asks, mirroring my thoughts. *I know she said she could, but no one has ever been rumored to forcibly be able to remove these chains.*

"I don't know," she replies quietly. "I just wanted them off."

She leans forward into my arms, giving me a hug. I wrap my arms around her and share a wide-eyed look with Esper.

"Have you ever seen that before?" I ask.

"Never," Esper responds faintly.

I shake off the shock and push out what bit of excess magic I still have to feel the surrounding area. I sense nothing immediate and ask Esper to check too. We both don't recognize anything waiting for us, so we pack up and leave to find some water. Since the air in Enelon has an unusual block to it, water is the strongest source to pull from.

While we walk, Esper falls into step beside me. "So," she starts, "you and Soren."

Nibbling at my bottom lip, I turn to her, "What do you mean?"

"I can tell there's something there," she says with a side grin.

Crimson stains my cheeks at the implication, I let my hair fall in front of my face, hiding my reaction.

"You're wrong. We barely tolerate each other," I say while looking at his back, not wanting to voice our fireside conversation. Esper notices my gaze, her smile widening.

"You should have seen him when you were passed out. He was very panicked," she tells me cheekily.

"You must be mistaken," I respond, unconvincingly. *If I admit it out loud, then it's something that can be ruined. I'm not ready for it to end.*

She makes a sound of disagreement. I go to answer her, but Soren turns around.

"How are you doing, princess?" he asks, his assessing gaze running over my body.

I clear my throat, hesitating. "I'm okay, thanks." Surprise flits through me as I think about my response. *It's the truth, I am okay. But I think a large part of that is because of him.* He nods at my answer, flashing me a charming smile before turning back around.

Esper lets out a snicker beside me. "Sure, nothing going on... princess."

I huff out a laugh and jokingly give her a shove.

About twenty minutes later, we come upon a small body of water, and I surge forward into it. I submerge myself, and a sense of calm washes over me as I feel my magic replenishing. I close my eyes and lean back, letting the small ripples run over me. Esper leaps in right after me.

I hear Poderosa scream, and my eyes snap open. I see Hock run out of the trees and grab Poderosa. Soren wrestles her away from him.

Everything happens so fast. As he hauls Poderosa away, Hock pulls out a knife, and before Soren can react, he shoves it through Soren's stomach.

I gasp, and my mind goes white with rage. My magic shoots out of me. The branches from a tree curl around Hock's body. Holding him. Soren falls to the ground, blood spilling from the wound. My panic and rage mix together, finding an outlet through my magic. I momentarily lose control, the branches tighten around Hock, crushing him. He screams in pain, the sound drowning out Poderosa's sobs. I quickly call my power back, and the branches release him.

He falls down, dead.

I rush over to Soren and place a bubble around the immediate area, not sensing any more of the men.

He's on his back when we get there, blood seeping out of him. I hold my hand over his stomach and put pressure on the wound. I feel a tear leak out of my eye as I try to think of what to do.

He tries to speak but coughs out some blood.

"You're okay, you're okay." I plead to him.

I hear Esper and Poderosa say something to me, but I tune them out.

My magic is not meant to heal at this scale, but I don't think about that. I just close my eyes and push everything I have into him. I feel my body hum with the amount of magic I'm using. I think of the wound closing and Soren sitting up. I think about us finding the cave of Orlo, freeing him from his blood oath.

I open my eyes and find the wound closed. The world seems to have taken on a silvery hue, but I ignore it, focusing on Soren. He lays still beneath my hands. I hold my breath, and a few seconds later, his chest moves. He takes a rattling breath, his hand reaching out weakly.

"Adira." He whispers.

I choke out a sob of disbelief. His eyes open.

I fall forward onto him, half out of relief, half out of dizziness. The only thing keeping me conscious is my adrenaline. A burning feeling lingers in my stomach, as if I absorbed some of his pain.

I lift my head to his face. His eyes are glassy.

"Princess," he croaks, "you're stunning."

He coughs feebly. The words seeming to steal his breath.

I sense the awe in his voice and feel my cheeks heat under his intense gaze.

Esper's astonished voice cuts through, "You're glowing, Adira."

"What?" I stutter, bringing my hand up. I notice a sheen silver aura surrounding it. It slowly fades while I stare down. Everyone is silent in shock.

Poderosa breaks the silence by jumping into Soren's arms.

I stand on shaky legs, forcing myself to stay conscious. Esper stands slowly with me.

"How did you do that?" she asks in shock.

"I have no idea," I reply honestly, surprise numbing my senses.

She stares at me a moment longer with wide eyes.

"That kind of magic isn't just rare—it's ancient. I've never seen anything like it. I've only read about similar magic in old books."

I shift uncomfortably, staring down at my hands. *What kind of magic was that?* I feel my pulse thrumming with a new energy. *Maybe my power has been gone for too long because of the Vormr. Maybe it just feels stronger, when in reality, it's the same as before.*

No, that can't be true.

"Or," she continues, "you and Soren could be true mates of heart. It's been rumored that true mates of heart can heal each other from critical injuries."

"No." I stammer out. "There's no way we are true mates of heart."

Soren winces as he pushes himself up onto his elbows. Arms shaking from the effort.

"What are true mates of heart?" He asks with an interested tone.

My cheeks redden as I wait for Esper to explain.

"They are very rare. Only a few have been recorded, so there is not much information on them. But it means you have found the person who makes your heart whole. When each person is at their highest power level, the Arae may bless a couple. Apparently, the sky clouds over and lightning strikes the couple. The strike doesn't hurt them, but they are left with a mark over their hearts and abilities unheard of."

I giggle uncomfortably. Soren has a bemused look on his face.

"See? No lightning strikes. We aren't true mates of heart."

Soren senses my discomfort and lets the conversation drop. His mind seems to turn over as he thinks about it.

"Thank you for the history lesson, Esper." I jokingly say. "But we need to go before they notice Hock is missing," I say, not wanting to dwell further on the fact that I was just a freaking glowworm or the terrifying topic of heart mates.

Soren shakingly pushes to his knees, his face alarmingly pale. I watch the slow movement with concern.

"Let's look for a cave. Soren needs to rest."

"I'm fine." He argues, his breathless voice giving him away.

"You almost died. You need to rest." I reply firmly.

"Okay." He concedes, quicker than he normally would. Concern floods me from his swift agreement.

Esper finds a cave nearby. I help Soren to his feet, walking slowly with him. When we finally reach the cave, he's on the verge of passing out. I unroll his bedding, and he collapses into it.

The rest of us settle in. I take first watch, staring out of the cave into the star filled sky. Wondering what I would have done if he didn't make it.

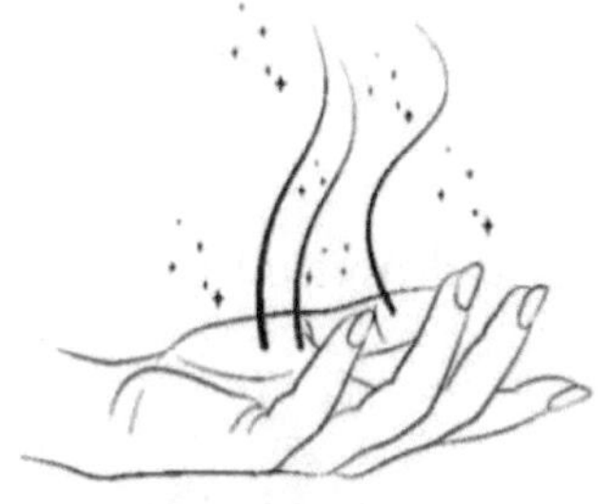

Chapter 19

Morning comes quickly. Soren stirs, his face showing more color. Heaving out a sigh of relief, I wake the others.

We pack up, walking to the entrance of the cave. Poderosa stops.

"I feel something."

"What do you feel?" I ask her.

"Power."

"Lead the way, Po." Soren says. My knees threaten to buckle at his casual tone. *He must be feeling a lot better.*

She leads us through the trees and onto an overgrown path. Vines coil around our legs as we push forward, the air growing thicker, heavier, as if the mountain itself is watching us. We are walking along it for a few minutes when we come up to a vast open area. She stops in front of it and just stares.

"What is it?" I ask her.

"I can feel it, but I don't know where it is." She says looking around.

We all split up and start checking out the area. Suddenly Soren shouts.

"Over here!"

We rush over to him and notice he's standing in front of a flatter part of the mountain.

"Up there." He points high and to the right.

We see the small symbol of Orlo. It's two daggers coming out of a skull. The skull's hollow eyes seem to glow a deep red. But it's only noticeable from a certain angle.

No wonder no one could find it. I think to myself.

Soren makes a move to climb up the rocks, but Esper puts her hand out, stopping him. He raises his eyebrow in question.

"You were at death's door yesterday. Let me do it." She states.

Before he can argue, she's expertly leaping onto the rocks, easily climbing them. Leaning over, she pushes the raised skull in.

A powerful wind whips around us as a low hum fills the air. Then, everything goes black. The world seems to spin. I panic as the floor drops out from under me, the sensation of free-falling rips a scream out of me.

The next instant, I blink, feeling a bit disoriented. I sit on a cold stone floor. The others lay scattered, looking dazed. I whip my head back and don't see the rolling hills that were all around us. I glance to the right and see a large cave opening. We must have been transported into the mountain.

I feel my smile growing as I realize we reached the entrance to the cave of Orlo.

***

We immediately start looking around, too excited to turn in for the night. There are patterns along the cave walls, not in a language any of us has heard of. We head deeper into the cave, following the markings on the wall. Running my hands along the images, I notice the wall is warm, as if pulsing with trapped energy. I push out my magic to capture a memory of the symbols. We continue walking, and the markings cover about fifty feet on each side of the gray walls. As we walk deeper into the cave, the air seems to press in on us, feeling heavier.

I notice Soren shifts closer to me as we walk, taking cautious steps. My eyebrows furrow. "What are you doing?" I ask.

He stays alert and says, "This is where I saw you die."

My body freezes as his words hit me.

"How did it happen?" I ask quietly.

"You drowned."

A tightness presses into my chest. My mind races back to the sting of almost drowning. The feeling of water closing in around me fills my senses. I shake away the panic, looking around for any signs of water.

I force a chuckle, but my fingers curl into fists.

"I think we should be okay, unless water comes shooting through the roof of the cave." I joke, trying to lighten the mood, even as fear threatens to smother me. The cave suddenly feels smaller, the air thick and damp, as if the water is already waiting for me.

Soren doesn't smile as he says, "Adira, we know what we saw. We aren't risking it."

My chest tightens at the protectiveness in his voice.

I just nod to him, emotion clogging my throat. Poderosa grabs my hand, and we continue walking forward, pausing every once in a while to try to make sense of the markings.

We come to a sharp bend in the cave and hear the distant sound of water falling. I feel the blood drain from my face. Soren tenses and wordlessly moves in front of me.

We start forward again at a slower pace and eventually reach an opening to a pool of water. I try to take a full breath, but the air is so stifling, it's difficult to breathe. Looking around for any signs of danger, I push my magic out for extra reassurance. Once I feel nothing, I let some of the tension ease from my body.

"I just won't get into the water." I say, forcing calmness into my voice. I glance wearily at the too still water, so smooth it looks like glass.

Just as Soren is about to answer, a giant gust of wind blows through the tunnel, pushing us all against the cave walls. The wind moves in front of us and forms the shape of a large human.

"Welcome to my oasis," the figure boasts.

"Who are you?" Soren demands as he pushes off the cave wall and steps toward it.

"I am Thaddeus. I was the first man to brave the realm of Orlo and made it this far before failing. My punishment was to be trapped in these caves forever."

Not sensing any immediate danger from Thaddeus, I take a step forward.

"How did you fail?" I ask loudly over the whistling wind.

"I could not take in the knowledge, it took me too deep," he replies.

My eyes dart to the water, a jolt of apprehension running through me.

"How do I avoid that?" I ask.

"I – open – need." His form flickers in and out as he speaks, as if he is trying to say more but is being restrained.

Disappointment filters through me at the lack of response. *I'm doomed.* I think to myself, trepidation trying to choke me.

"I can tell you this," he continues. "To reveal the lost message of Orlo, the one who bound the group together must venture into the depths of the water and open the mind."

A shudder rolls through me, and I close my eyes. *You can do this. The visions may still be wrong. You could still make it out alive.*

Nausea takes root. *I don't want to die today.*

When I open my eyes, Soren is right in front of me, looking at me with concern in his blue eyes. He grips my wrist tightly.

"No," his voice desperate, breaking.

"I have to," I say with forced determination. *Right?* I ask myself, my mind trying to find any alternative. My courage falters at the emotion in his eyes.

"Maybe...maybe the visions were wrong. Maybe I won't...I won't," my voice trembles, I stop speaking, unable to voice the word *die*.

"Are you insane? There's no way the vision doesn't come true," he half-shouts at me, fear mixing with his agitation. I swallow thickly at the conviction in his voice.

A shockwave of trepidation rolls through me as I take a step back from Soren.

"You aren't making this any easier," I cry out to him. "We get nowhere if I don't go into that water."

I could still make it out. I repeat to myself over and over again. Willing myself to believe it.

"What if I went instead?" He pleads with me.

Heart clenching at the offer, I shake my head. "You know you can't. It has to be me. I started this."

He stands there with his eyes closed, chest rising and falling as he tries to get a hold of his emotions. A second later, his eyes snap open, and he crosses the space between us in two long strides.

He grabs me around the waist and pulls me to him. My lips part in shock, and in a heartbeat, I feel his soft lips crush into mine.

I melt into him as he deepens the kiss. I lift my hands to his hair and pull his head down to me, trying to get him as close as possible.

A moment later, he pulls back, exhaling roughly. His forehead falls to mine, and he meets my eyes through his hair. His eyes are full of promises of what could have been. He closes his eyes, and when he opens them again, I see his resolve, along with a touch of guilt.

I wonder what he feels guilty about, I think to myself.

It must be that I have to do all the tasks alone, I reason in my head.

"I'm not ready to say goodbye." He admits quietly.

My hands slide down his arms, grasping his hands. I squeeze them lightly. "Then don't. It's not over yet."

"Come back to me."

I gulp down the flood of emotions threatening to suffocate me. Staying silent, I shoot him a small smile, not wanting to make promises I can't keep.

I take a breath in with the reality of what's next and take a step back from Soren on shaky legs.

I put one hand against the cave wall and close my eyes, catching my breath. After a moment, I push off and walk over to Poderosa and Esper.

Esper's eyes are raised to her brows. "I'm not going to tease you about what just happened because you may potentially die."

A laugh escapes me. I clear my throat and look back at Esper.

"I wish we met sooner. You've quickly become one of my favorite people," I confess.

Her eyes take on a glassy sheen. "We'll have more time. We still need to wreak havoc on the world with our air magic."

I lean forward and give her a hug. "Make sure they get out of here," I whisper to her.

I pull back and crouch down to Poderosa. I feel the wetness behind my eyes as I see hers wide with fear. I open my arms, and she leaps into them.

"It's okay," I tell her, hugging her tightly.

"Please don't go." She begs me with a shaking voice.

"I have to. I am so sorry." I say thickly, emotion clogging my throat.

She pulls back, gripping my sleeves with her small hands.

"But I want you to stay."

My heart cracks.

"I know. I want to stay too."

"But, if I don't come back," I choke out, "I want you to stick with Soren, okay? He will take care of you."

She nods with tears in her eyes, then leaps back into my arms, hugging me tightly.

A minute goes by, and I slowly peel her away from me, handing her over to Soren's waiting arms.

I walk toward the edge of the water, when I'm a step away, my feet stop. Body resisting. My power hums deep inside, as if warning me this is a bad idea.

I turn back to them one more time.

"You guys are going to be okay," I state.

"But I'm going to miss you," I say with a watery smile.

I stop at the water's edge, taking a deep breath. Just before I step in, a voice floats to me.

"Not all who drown, die."

Uncertainty flickers through me at the conflicting statement.

I step into the water. As soon as I touch it, whispers fill my mind, hushed voices that carry warning tones. I resist the urge to bolt out of the water, Vormr be damned.

Ignoring them as much as I can, I tread into the water until I'm about waist-deep.

I take a deep breath and before my mind can convince me that this is a terrible idea, I dive in.

Immediately, a surge of images flash into my mind. Each one coming so fast, making it hard to focus on only one. The swiftness blends with the pressure of the water, causing my head to throb.

A stream of water wraps around my ankle like a hand. It tugs at me, dragging me deeper. My lungs start to burn as some of the image's flash brighter than others. A twisted crown resting on a blood-red throne, a dark world with layers of beasts, and a malicious god ruling over a ruined world. A scream bursts out of me, bubbles floating to the surface as the pressure threatens to implode. I start to see black dots in my vision and slowly lose consciousness.

***

Up on the surface, Soren, Esper, and Poderosa stand at the edge of the water, waiting anxiously for Adira to emerge. After several minutes without seeing even a ripple, they start to lose hope. Poderosa cries out, holding a hand up. She releases a burst of power toward Adira, but it ricochets off the smooth water, bouncing off the cave walls. Her sobs get louder at the failed rescue attempt.

Poderosa goes over to Soren, wrapping her arms around him. They silently grieve for Adira, already knowing her fate before she entered the water.

After a few more moments, Esper breaks the silence.

"I think she's gone." She croaks out, disbelief in her voice. As if she is telling herself as much as the others.

Soren shoots her a sharp look.

"How can you say that?"

"No one can survive that long in the water." She states despondently.

Soren ignores her, refusing to give up. He paces the edge of the water, looking out for any sign of Adira.

Another minute ticks by.

Then another.

The hope deflates out of Soren. A sullen look takes over his features.

Then, a light, shaking sound comes from the water.

Soren's heart hitches, and he whips around. The water glows blue, getting brighter as something rushes to the surface.

The surface breaks, a man shoots out, carrying Adira like a fallen goddess.

He drops down onto the hard ground, setting Adira down gently.

Soren rushes forward to the unconscious Adira. Drawing his sword against the man. Esper calls upon her magic, letting it hover in the air in preparation.

The man quirks an eyebrow, then smirks, unbothered. He waves a hand lightly through the air. The sword goes flying out of Soren's grasp just as Esper's magic dissipates.

Esper's jaw drops as Soren pauses his attack.

"Who are you?" Soren demands of the man.

"I'm Cade. Ruler of the Laic Kingdom," he states strongly, his voice captivating.

"Are you going to harm her?" Soren asks harshly.

"Or us?" Esper squeaks out from behind him.

He smirks again.

"No. I am not here to harm anyone."

Soren's eyes catch on Adira's unmoving body and decides that he has to trust him for now. Stepping over to her, he bends down, grasping her cold hand. He starts to panic when he notices that she isn't breathing. Cade crouches down next to her and places his hand on Adira's forehead.

Soren starts to object but stops himself when he notices a light blue glow coming from Cade's hand.

A second later, Adira coughs out water. She turns on her side, spewing out the rest of the water. When she's done, Soren grabs her into a hug and exhales a shaky breath of relief.

***

When I'm down puking up half the lake, I look around me, trying to focus on my surroundings. The magic from the water still buzzing through my system, making me feel unsteady. An attractive man with long dark hair and tan skin stands over me. Soren pulls me tighter to his chest, and I sag against him. Poderosa jumps forward and wraps her small arms around both of us. Esper grins down at us from above.

My mind catches up to my body, and I start to remember everything I saw down there.

The images that were thrown at me are now easily reachable in my mind. I close my eyes and focus on them, noticing that each one plays out like an echo of a memory, showing me exactly what each marking on the wall means.

I pull back slightly from Soren and look up at the mystery man, realizing how I'm still alive.

"Thank you," I say to him softly, my voice raspy.

He tilts his head forward at me in acknowledgment.

"What's your name?" I ask him.

"Cade," he says simply. His green eyes pierce into mine.

A man of few words, I think to myself.

I open my mouth to ask him more questions, but he leans in closer, speaking first.

"This isn't our last meeting, Adira." he says mysteriously stepping back toward the water. "Until next time."

He sinks gracefully into the water. His last words ringing through my head.

I share a look with Soren. "That was strange. I wonder what he meant by 'until next time.'"

"Let's not worry about that now," Soren says as he tightens his grip around me.

"Did you tell him my name?" I ask.

Soren frowns, eyes shifting toward the water.

"No, I didn't."

Uneasiness settles inside me.

"Where did he come from?"

Soren just shrugs.

"He said he is the Ruler of the Laic Kingdom."

My body freezes at his words. He keeps going, unbothered.

"I assume it's a place in Modereo, since he has magic."

Esper has a look of concentration on her face, as if she is trying to remember the geography of Modereo.

"That place isn't in Modereo." I tell Soren.

His eyes widen slightly at the news.

"He must be from another world." I ponder out loud. Shock settles into me as I think about it. The Arae could've created multiple worlds, if the history books are correct, they became uninterested in their creations quickly. Nerves nestle into me at the thought of seeing him again. *I don't want to go to another world, I can barely handle this one.* I think with horror.

I push everything out of my mind and focus on the others. We silently prepare for the night and lay down side by side. We fall asleep with an air of relief that we are all alive and well.

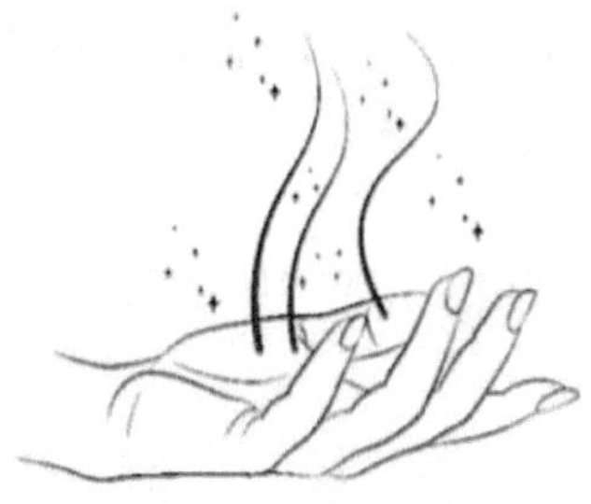

Chapter 20

I wake in the morning feeling refreshed. After sifting through the memories that were shoved into my brain, I understand why this is so closely protected. I ignore the immediate anger from my new knowledge, choosing to deal with it later.

As the others begin to stir, I get up and start packing our supplies.

"We need to head northwest," I tell them.

"What about the cave translations?" Soren asks.

My mind flashes through the images, getting stuck on the three prominent visions. A twisted crown resting on a blood-red throne, a dark world with layers of beasts, and a malicious god ruling over a ruined world.

I open my mouth to reply, but a bolt of energy shoots through me, as if warning me to stay silent.

"I think." I start slowly. "They have to remain a secret for now. I assume that's part of the test. We just need to focus on the last task."

A stab of unease fills me at the thought of keeping this from them.

Soren notices.

"Are you certain you can't tell us anything?" A hint of suspicion in his eyes.

"It won't let me. The magic from it physically stops me from speaking of it."

Soren reluctantly nods in understanding, and we all head out.

The weight of the cave's secrets presses down on me, making me feel restless. *I know people say that knowledge is power, but this knowledge makes me feel like the morality of the world is hanging by a string.*

We walk back through the cave and emerge onto a windy path along the edge of the mountain. This must be the way out. The air seems to have a slight charge to it, gradually increasing as we walk.

Esper and I lead the pack as we turn corner after corner.

"I'm glad you're alive," she states. "Now I can tease you more about Soren." She grins devilishly.

"I—" I begin, but a loud crash behind us cuts me off.

I spin and see a large rock in the middle of the path, separating Soren and Poderosa on the other side. My heart pounds as I put a hand to my chest. That's when I notice the air has stilled, no sign of the energy swirling through it.

"What was that abou—" My words die in my throat as two men appear around the corner.

Damn, I can't even finish a sentence here. I think with frustration.

Esper and I meet their swords with our own. I pull on my magic—but nothing happens. My stomach drops. I try again, but I feel nothing. Horror grasps me from the loss of my magic. My brain spins, trying to make sense of it. Only one conclusion comes to mind.

Shit, we must be in a dead zone.

Esper realizes it at the same time I do.

"I guess we just need to deal with this the regular way," she says with a grin.

I just shake my head at her enthusiasm and dodge the man's sword. The edge of the cliff dangerously beckons me. My mind flashes back to the vision from the crystal orb. Alarm flickers.

"Stay away from the edge." I shout to Esper.

She nods to me in understanding.

From the other side of the rock, Soren shouts, trying to find a way through. Out of the corner of my eye, I see Esper slice through her opponent's gut.

Then, pain.

My body jerks, and I look down in confusion. An arrow juts out of my thigh. It goes numb and I fall to the side, toppling over the edge of the cliff.

"Adira!" Esper's scream rings in my ears.

Desperately, I reach out with my sword-free hand, grabbing the cliff's edge. My fingers scrape against jagged rock. Gritting my teeth, I sheath my sword and reach out with my other hand. Holding tight to the uneven rocks I clutch the ledge with both hands, my arms trembling under the strain. Images replay in my mind, accompanied with the feeling of death. My jaw clenches painfully as I grasp tighter to the stone, refusing to die.

Esper disarms the remaining man and runs over to me, dropping her sword as she reaches down to pull me up. I get one forearm on solid ground, a foot wedged into a crevice.

Then, she jolts.

Horror grips me as a sword pierces through her chest. She falls forward, tumbling over me. A scream rips through my throat as I watch her plunge, helpless, to the rocky terrain below.

No, no, no, no, this can't be happening.

A strangled sound escapes me—half-scream, half-sob. My mind blanks, consumed by disbelief.

Steel clashes. A grunt. I barely register Soren slicing the man's neck before he rushes to me. He hauls me up in one swift motion.

I try to focus on what's happening. "There's a man with a bow and arrow," I manage, my voice hoarse.

"I know," Soren says grimly. "I found him when I was scaling over the rocks to this side."

I nod numbly. My gaze drifts over the cliff's edge.

"She's gone." My voice cracks.

Soren pulls me into a tight embrace.

"I know, sweetheart."

"She's gone because she saved me," I whisper.

His arms tense around me.

"Then I will forever be thankful to her," he promises out loud.

Tears carve hot trails down my cheeks as Soren rubs my back.

This is my fault.

I don't know how much time passes before I pull away.

"I guess we should get moving," I mutter, glancing sheepishly in Poderosa's direction. She looks solemn as she stares at us.

"Is she going to come back?" She asks quietly.

I choke on a sob.

Soren answers her. "No, Po, she isn't."

She lets out a quiet sob as she walks over to us. I gather her in a hug, and we cry together. After a few moments, I straighten up, the urge to get off this cliff overwhelming.

"Let's go."

"Are you sure you're okay to keep going? We can rest for a while," Soren says gently.

I clear my throat, pushing away my thoughts. "I'm sure. I can't be here any longer."

Moving to stand up, pain flares in my leg, I slump back to the ground.

Soren's concerned gaze moves over my body.

"Your leg. What happened?"

"Got hit with an arrow." I reply, grimacing at the blood still pouring out.

"Can you heal yourself?" Soren asks.

"No. We are in a dead zone. Which means I can't summon magic here."

"Shit. I didn't know those existed." He says, ripping a piece of fabric from his shirt. "We'll wrap it for now and hopefully be out of this dead zone soon."

"Thanks." I mutter.

I hiss in pain as he wraps it tight, staunching the blood flow.

"Sorry." He murmurs as he ties it off. He helps me stand, slinging an arm around my waist. I lean into his strength, and we start forward, Poderosa following beside us silently.

We only have to walk for about ten minutes before the flow of magic trickles back into me. Sighing in relief, I push it towards my thigh, closing the wound.

"My magic is back. The wound is closed now." I tell Soren, straightening up and away from him.

"Good." He replies, the relief evident on his face. Poderosa gives me a small smile before focusing on the path, seeming lost in thought.

She liked Esper. This must be hard for her. I wish I could comfort her, but I barely feel like I'm holding on myself.

The next day passes in a blur as we wind our way down the mountain. Poderosa keeps glancing behind her, as if Esper will appear. Soren tries to talk to me, but I stay silent, declining to respond. When we finally reach level ground, we set up camp for the night. Poderosa crawls into my bed with me, snuggling in close. My brain is too muddled to offer words of comfort, so I welcome the nothingness that sleep offers.

Morning comes, but it doesn't feel like it should. Sleep may have claimed me, but it did nothing to quiet the echo of Esper's last scream.

"How are you doing, princess?" Soren asks gently.

I barely acknowledge his question. Letting out a half-human noncommittal sound.

Two more days pass in a haze. A thick mist rolls in, making the forest seem haunted. I keep flinching as we walk, certain I see Esper between the trees. I feel Soren's worried gaze on me, but I don't reassure him that I'm fine.

Because you're not fine. I admit to myself.

On the fourth day, we reach the Town of Ayward, a small town that borders the water. I look ahead to its dark buildings and eerie atmosphere, letting the danger emitting from it sharpen my senses.

As we near the edge of the village, my mother's voice echoes in my mind:

Distraction will kill you. You always need to be alert. No matter what happens. People will die, and you will need to deal with it. Quickly.

I try to heed her words and shake myself out of my grief, forcing myself to scan our surroundings.

Feeling weary from four days of travel, we decide to rest for the night at an inn.

Soren and I keep a close eye on the townsfolk as we slip into the dimly lit tavern. After a quick meal, we head upstairs. I push out my power, setting up a protective ward around the room for Poderosa. She lays onto the bed, her face glum. I go over to her, grabbing her hand.

"We will be back soon, okay? Get some rest."

"Will you come back?" Her voice cracks.

I blink back tears at the heartbroken question.

"I promise. We will come back."

She nods, burrowing into the pillow.

Once she settles in, Soren and I go out to search for supplies.

"Sorry for the last few days," I say quietly.

His relief is palpable.

I hesitate. "I need to be back. I need to move forward. But a part of me is still falling off that cliff with Esper." My voice revealing the numbness I still feel.

He grabs my hand. Enclosing it in his when he realizes how cold it is. Warmth floods into me from his touch.

"I don't need you to tell me you're okay, Adira. I need you to let me in."

"I just need things to feel like they are back to normal," I admit.

He sighs as I blatantly refuse to acknowledge my feelings.

"Okay. I can do that." Soren clears his throat. "I saw an area of small vendor stands in the town square. We need to replenish our supplies before we keep going." My eyes skim over the weathered buildings that line the street, most seeming abandoned. The street is quiet, the sound of children laughing absent from the peculiar town. Only a handful of people walk along the main road, they all look at us with mistrust.

I nod warily, tearing my gaze away from their guarded stares. "Let's do it quickly and get some rest."

He nods in agreement, stopping me before I can turn away.

"Be careful, princess. There's something odd about this town."

"I feel it too." I agree. His eyes drop to my lips, and he steps forward. My pulse quickens. He stops himself, clearing his throat.

"Okay, I'll be quick."

I watch him head off, startled that the small interaction sparked something in me. Making me feel more normal than I have felt in days.

While he heads to the vendors, I walk to the edge of the water, scanning for ways to get across. My gaze lands on a man stationed at an isolated booth, selling weapons. Something about the booth's placement and the man's demeanor sets him apart from the others. I make my way over, pretending to browse the selection laid out in front of me.

A small dagger with an oak handle catches my eye. I pick it up, weighing it in my hand. It's well-balanced, the blade sharp.

"I'll take it," I say.

The man watches me for a moment before nodding. "Wise choice," he replies gruffly, wrapping it up.

As he works, I take the chance to ask, "Can you tell me how I can charter a boat?"

"Sure thing. Most folks here have a boat." He glances at me. "Hell, I have one I can charter out. Where are you headed?"

"The Island of Harnew," I state.

His hands still. When he looks up, his expression is unreadable, but his eyes hold a flicker of something—fear?

I notice another patron turn silent, walking away swiftly.

He lowers his voice, looking around nervously.

"No soul has ever come back from that island," he says. "Why the hell would you want to go there?"

"That's my business," I answer firmly.

He shakes his head. "Well, I won't do it. There's no way my boat is coming back if you take it there."

He keeps rambling. "Many of the locals have tried, and none have returned. The legend says that when you enter the chamber, it swallows you with its thoughts. You never want to come out."

I frown. "You don't *want* to? Not that you *can't* come out?"

He nods. "That's what the stories all say."

I hesitate, considering his words. A place that keeps people by making them *want* to stay? I push down the unease curling in my stomach.

"I'll pay ten Ellyr," I say quickly.

He shakes his head. "Not worth it. And you should really consider if it's worth it going to that place."

"Twenty Ellyr." I counter. "One way or another, I am getting to that island."

He eyes me again, sensing my resolve, "Make it double."

"Done."

We shake hands, and I hand over the payment for the dagger.

"We leave at first light. Will you be ready?" I ask.

"Sure thing." He jerks his thumb toward the docks. "That dark blue boat over there—that's the one we'll be taking."

I glance at it. It looks sturdy enough. "Great. We'll see you first thing, then."

Turning away, I head back towards Soren and find him already walking towards me with a bag of supplies slung over his shoulder. I take the moment to watch him. His dark hair is swept sideways from the wind. His pants tighten around his thighs as his muscles shift. I draw my eyes up to his penetrating gaze.

He nods at the dagger in my hand. "What's that for?"

"Just for fun." I reply.

He snickers. "Of course you would get a weapon for *fun.*"

"What can I say? I like how it feels in my hand." I wink back.

He chuckles, and a lazy grin flits across his face.

I smirk. "I got us a boat. We leave at first light."

His eyebrows shoot up. "I was gone for five minutes, and you already secured us passage?"

I shrug and start walking in the direction of the inn.

Before I can take another step, Soren grabs my arm and pulls me into a nearby alley. My back presses against the cool brick wall, and before I can react, his mouth crashes onto mine.

"It's so attractive when you take charge," he murmurs, desire burning in his eyes.

My body throbs at his dominant gesture. I fist the front of his shirt, yanking him closer as I claim his lips again.

He hikes my leg up, pressing himself against me, and I groan as I feel his hard length. I lift my leg higher to grant him better access.

He pauses, searching my eyes.

I pull him closer and rasp in his ear, "Don't you dare stop."

A deep growl rumbles in his throat. His hand reaches down, and in one swift motion, he pulls himself out. He grabs my underwear, tearing it away. I feel the tip of him line up with me. The sudden exposure sends a shiver down my entrance and then my spine.

Then, he pushes into me.

I gasp at the intrusion, my body adjusting to the stretch. Slowly, I roll my hips, coaxing him deeper.

Soren groans, his hands gripping my waist as my body gets used to it.

He starts slowly pumping into me, the friction becoming overwhelming. Soren grabs my hips and starts moving at a faster rhythm. I feel the heat build in me and grab onto his back to keep myself upright. I groan at the shift.

I hear voices passing by the alleyway entrance and snap my mouth shut to muffle my noises.

Soren hears them too.

Footsteps echo near the alley's entrance. Voices murmur.

My eyes widen, and I bite my lip, stifling the moan threatening to escape.

Soren smirks, his breath hot against my ear. "You better be quiet if you don't want to get caught." He taunts.

I say nothing, but my body betrays me, tightening around him at the thrill of being seen. He feels it.

"You'd like that, wouldn't you?" He groans. "Too bad. Only I get to see you like this."

He keeps pounding me into the cold brick wall. I start to come undone at the feverish look in his eyes.

His thrusts grow sharper, each one pushing me closer to the edge. His fevered gaze locks onto mine, and I unravel beneath him.

"That's it," he murmurs. "Let go. Come on my dick." He whispers in my ear breathlessly.

My head falls back with my release, taking me under. A moment later, Soren shudders, finding his own release with a deep, guttural sound.

For a moment, neither of us moves. Our bodies are slack, pressed against each other, breathing hard.

I try not to let my mind stray to thoughts of how soon the end of the journey is. Reality creeps in. The night air cools my heated skin.

Soren gently pulls out of me, lowering my leg to the ground. We adjust our clothes, and I press a final kiss to his lips before stepping away.

We walk back to the inn, an air of comfortable silence settling around us. He grabs my hand as we walk, pulling me closer to him. I stumble a bit to the side, closing the distance. We walk side by side, but he doesn't take his hand back. An unknown feeling of contentment flows through me. I smile up at him, letting the feeling dull the numbness of grief.

When we reach our room, I ease the door open, careful not to wake Poderosa. She's out cold. Dried tears cover her cheeks. My heart breaks for her and I vow to myself that I will be better for her.

Soren places the supplies in our packs as I climb into bed, exhaustion seeping into my bones. I feel Soren's gaze on me, turning to him I notice his eyebrows are drawn together, he's looking at me as if he's worried we won't get many more moments like tonight. I turn onto my back, staring at the ceiling, the weight of grief catching up to me. An empty feeling takes root. I sigh to myself, wondering how long the feeling of hollowness will last.

A moment later, the mattress dips as Soren slides in beside me, pulling me against his chest. His warmth is grounding.

I relax in his arms, close my eyes and let sleep take me.

Chapter 21

A prickle creeps along the back of my neck, waking me. The air is thick, charged with something unseen. I sit up, instantly alert. Slipping out of bed, I move quietly to the window, my pulse already quickening.

Outside, under the dim glow of lanterns, I spot a small group of guards speaking with the innkeeper. The innkeeper has an indecisive look on his face. One of the guards pulls out a handful of Ellyr, offering it to him. The innkeeper greedily takes the coin, gesturing to the rooms above. Our rooms.

"Shit," I mutter.

I turn away and see Soren stirring. Wasting no time, I cross the room to him.

"We need to go. Now."

He doesn't hesitate. He throws off the blankets and starts grabbing our belongings.

I move to Poderosa's bed, crouching beside her. "Wake up, hon. We need to go." My voice is soft but urgent.

She blinks, disoriented, then sees the seriousness in my expression. Without a word, she sits up and hurriedly pulls on her boots.

Less than a minute later, we slip out the back door of the inn, our movements swift and silent. Footsteps sound, we pause, backing into the shadows just as a guard comes around the corner.

My heart pounds against my ribs frantically. I hold Poderosa back, waiting for the perfect moment to move.

The guard comes closer. I call up a shield, obscuring us from sight. He stops near us, glancing around as if he feels something off. Holding our breath, we wait for him to move on. A sense of urgency takes hold. *We need to get out of here before they find our empty room.*

Finally, he shrugs the feeling off, striding forward and stopping in front of the door we came out of a minute before. I keep the shield on all of us, motioning the other's forward. Keeping our steps silent, we increase the distance between him and us. Reaching the end of the alley, we turn the corner.

Letting out a breath of relief, I drop the shield.

The night air is cool, thick with the scent of salt and damp wood. I look around, scanning the shadows for any sign of pursuit. The muffled voices of the guards grow louder.

We rush toward the docks, our steps light but quick. The dark blue boat waits where the man had left it, an unusual brisk air surrounding it. The boat creaks loudly, even as the water around it sits still. I shake off the eerie feeling, blaming it on the equally eerie town. Soren and I work swiftly to untie it. I drop the agreed forty Ellyr onto the dock, hoping he'll find it come morning.

Poderosa climbs in first, followed by Soren. I push us off, the wooden hull slicing through the black water. The night feels too silent, as if the sea itself is holding its breath.

As we row quietly into the dark water, we hear the shouts of guards echo through the town.

I exhale slowly, my breath unsteady. The shoreline fades into darkness behind us. The light of the moon draws my attention, I follow it down to the water. Frowning, when I see that the moonlight on the water doesn't ripple, like the reflection is frozen in place. *You knew there was going to be some ancient magic involved in these tasks.* I remind myself. But a shiver rolls up my spine, because this one feels the most unsettling.

Focusing my attention up front, I stare into the night. Nothing but open water awaits, along with the final task of our journey.

***

As the first light of dawn stretches across the sky, it casts a golden glow over the water.

"It's so beautiful," I breathe, staring at the horizon.

"Yes, it is," Soren agrees.

When I turn to him, he's not looking at the view—he's looking at me. I feel the heat rise to my cheeks under the weight of his gaze.

"Smooth talker," I say with a grin.

He smirks but says nothing, simply continuing to row.

The waves feel unnatural as we move through them. It is almost as if they are pulling us in the direction of the island. Glancing at the sky, I notice there is no wind. I shake off the sense of foreboding, choosing to delight in the morning sun.

By early afternoon, the island appears in the distance, a dark silhouette against the vast blue. By nightfall, we are almost upon it.

"The sky looks wrong here." Poderosa says into the silence.

We glance up. The stars seem to get bigger the closer we get to the island. Tilting my head, I eye them curiously. *I've never seen that before. Maybe they aren't stars.* I shake that thought away quickly, having no idea what else they would be.

After a few more minutes, we reach the shore.

Soren jumps out first, the water sloshing around his legs as he pulls the boat onto the sand. Poderosa and I climb out, our feet sinking into the soft ground.

The island is dense with towering green trees, their thick foliage parting just enough to reveal a narrow path. In the distance, I glimpse a piece of a stone structure, weathered by time. A calming sensation filters through me. Chasing away my worries about the mystifying island.

Faint whispers cut through the trees. I turn in the direction but see nothing. An alarm signals deep within me. I shake off the comfort that threatens to encompass me again.

I inhale deeply, my mind replaying the local man's warning. *No one has ever returned. But not because they can't leave—because they don't want to.*

A chill runs down my spine. *What could possibly be inside that chamber?*

Why wouldn't I want to leave? What's on the other side of the door? I think grimly.

We make camp at the tree line and settle in for the night.

***

I wake before dawn, feeling the weight of what's ahead. I peer at the others and realize they're already awake too.

No words are needed. We gather our things in silence and step onto the path, moving deeper into the island's heart.

As we walk, the branches seem to shift slightly, following our movements. It is almost as if they are watching us pass. I glance back, but find the path overgrown. Swallowing down my unease, I try not to think about what would happen if we decided to turn back. *Would the island let us?*

By midday, we reach the sealed entrance to the chamber. The stone surface is covered in ancient carvings—warnings, perhaps. At the center, an inscription makes the method of entry clear: *Blood must be spilled to open the way.*

Soren steps forward without hesitation. "Let me do it."

"You know you can't." I shake my head. "I started these tasks, and I have to finish them." I remind him of the forewarning told to us.

His jaw tightens. "I've been with you for all three tasks. Maybe it will let me do this one?"

"I doubt it, and I don't want to risk it." A tone of finality in my voice. The thought of coming this far, only to fail, is unbearable.

"I don't like this." He says while looking around.

I glance around at the dense, ominous forest, as if expecting something—or someone—to emerge.

I force a small shrug, ignoring the unease clawing at my own gut. "It'll be fine."

His expression darkens. "The stories say that those who enter don't come out." He exhales sharply, running a hand through his hair as he relays what I told him. "I don't know what's waiting for you in there, but if—" His voice catches, and he starts again. "If you don't come out, we will find a way in. I don't care what the legends say—I will tear this place apart if you don't come out."

I swallow hard, willing my voice to stay steady. "If something happens, you *have* to go."

Soren is already shaking his head. "We aren't going to leave you."

He pulls me against him, pressing his forehead to mine, staring down at me like he's memorizing me. "You'll be fine, you're strong." He murmurs, his eyes closed like he's convincing himself. "We've made it this far. We're *all* going to make it to the end."

Dipping his head down, he crushes his lips to mine. A sense of desperation in the kiss. Like he's saying goodbye. He pulls back, locking eyes with me.

"You have to come back, Adira. Not for this mission—for me."

My heart flutters in response.

"I will." I promise. Hoping that I can keep it.

I barely manage to pull away before Poderosa crashes into me. Her arms wrap tightly around my waist.

I hug her back, pressing a kiss to her head. "Take care of him while I'm in there, okay? *Don't* let him come after me."

She nods, though tears glisten in her eyes. I start to pull away, but she clings onto me, refusing to let go.

No matter how many times I say goodbye, it's never any easier.

"I'll be okay." I promise her, because what's one more promise. She reluctantly let's go, wiping her tears away with the back of her hand. My heart breaks at the sight. *She's cried more than a child ever should. I hope we can find a place for her to live happily after this.* I hesitate on the 'we'. *Or I hope Soren can.*

Steeling myself, I unsheathe my new dagger. The blade is cool against my palm as I press it to my skin, but my body pauses. Fear trickles in as I look up at the cryptic chamber, terrified about what one drop of blood could do. A hint of faint laughter echoes from inside. I freeze, straining my ears, but the only sound is the wind whistling. Pushing through the fear, I slice through my hand quickly. A thin line of crimson wells up before dripping into the stone bowl carved into the door. The blood vanishes instantly, as if the chamber swallowed it.

For a moment, nothing happens. Then—

A loud crack shatters the silence. The door groans, as if something primitive is waking. Rumbling shakes the ground as it shifts open.

I turn back one last time. Soren's expression is unreadable, but his fists are clenched. Poderosa grips his arm as if holding him back.

I lift a hand in farewell and step inside.

The door shuts quickly once I step over the threshold, plunging me into pitched darkness. A feeling of trepidation takes over, as if warning me that I was never supposed to enter.

I take a small step forward. Two small torches flicker to life, casting an eerie glow. I walk further down the dim hall, the torches igniting one by one as I pass, following my movements like eyes snapping open.

A heartbeat bounces off the walls, pulsing loudly. I press a hand to my chest in confusion. The beat not matching. The hair on my arms stands up.

A long, narrow hallway stretches before me, ending with a single door. I inhale sharply, my pulse pounding in my ears.

I cautiously walk towards it, when I'm about a foot away, the door creaks open.

I hesitate.

Then, squaring my shoulders, I step through.

A sharp gasp escapes me, echoing in the chamber.

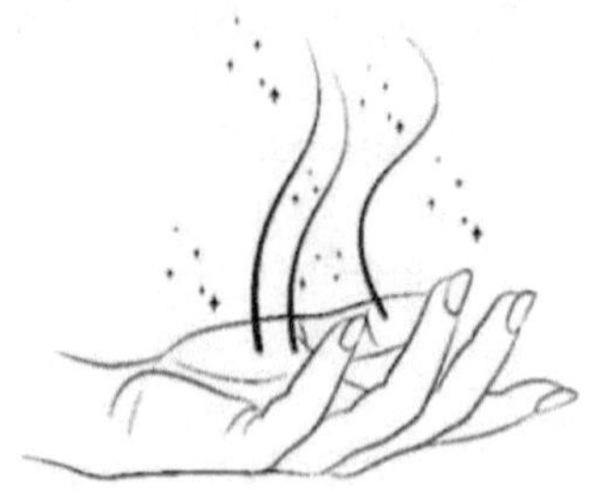

Chapter 22

I see my friends sitting at a table in the center of the room. When they hear me enter, they turn with bright smiles. Their faces faintly blur, my body sways as I try to focus. Blinking rapidly, their friendly expressions sharpen. Relief rushes through me, but something...something feels off. I shake that thought away.

"Come sit with us, Adira!"

"We missed you."

Their voices overlap slightly, making it sound like the words are delayed. *That's strange.*

The still air rushes over me, leaving me feeling lighter. A smile overtakes my face as a strong feeling of peace wraps around me.

Tears spring to my eyes. I give them a watery smile. "I missed you too."

I rush to them, wrapping my arms around each of them in turn. Their warmth is familiar, comforting. I sit down, and we fall into easy conversation, talking about every little thing.

"Show us the new spell you learned yesterday, Adira!" Saline says eagerly.

My smile falters. "I can't. My magic is depleted."

They both look at me, concern creasing their brows.

"What? Why would it be depleted?"

A strange fuzziness clouds my mind. I try to recall the reason—try to remind them why but can't seem to remember.

I glance inward, checking my magic reserves. They're full.

Confused, a faint sense of unease sneaks in. I close my eyes, trying to remember why. Invisible claws scratch at my mind, demanding to tear into my skull. They get faster, weakening my barrier. A sharp pain shoots through my head, blasting my control away.

"I should be happy. I am happy. So why does it feel like something is clawing at the edges of my mind, begging me to wake up?" I whisper to myself.

I push the thought aside as we take turns showing each other our favorite spells. Laughter fills the air, and for a moment, everything feels perfect.

After a while, Saline leans in with a smirk. "So... when's your *new man* coming to meet us?"

My brow furrows. "What?"

Before I can process the question, a familiar voice speaks from behind me.

"Sorry I'm late, princess."

I turn in shock as Soren strolls in, effortlessly sliding into the scene. He leans down, pressing a kiss to my head. "It's nice to finally meet you, Saline. And you, Atin."

I tense at his kiss. Leaning away instinctively. *Why did I do that? Did I tell him their names?*

My brain spins as I attempt to retrieve those memories.

He sits next to me, pulling me into his side. His touch relaxing me, causing my uncertainty to fade away.

I look around the table. They're talking. Laughing.

A warmth fills my chest, a burst of pure happiness. Everything is **right**.

Then—

"I can't believe you guys started without me!"

The voice makes my stomach drop.

I whip around. A rush of cold air settles over me, chilling me.

"Esper!" I gasp out.

Stumbling to my feet, I rush over to her. She opens her arms for a hug, but before I step into the embrace, I hesitate. My body stopping before her. My stomach twists. I force my feet forward, returning her hug stiffly.

"I'm so glad you're here," I whisper. "I've missed you. I can't believe you di—"

The words stick in my throat.

Died.

I was going to say *died.*

But that can't be right. Esper is here. She's standing right in front of me.

Esper tilts her head. Her smile widens, but her eyes stay blank. "I'm so glad you're here too."

Anxiety blossoms at her blank eyes.

A gust of air flows over me. My mind quiets. A soothing feeling washes through me.

I sit back down, snuggling back into Soren's warmth. We talk for hours, losing ourselves in the joy of the reunion.

Soren's teasing voice makes me turn my attention to him.

"As much as I hate to admit it. Adira can best me in a fight. It's true, I'm not lying. She's already done it."

I laugh along with the rest of them but pause at his words. Not remembering the moment he is talking about. Doubt seeps in. *Is it true? Or is it just what I want to hear?*

I push the thought away. *No. Soren wouldn't admit to that if it weren't true.*

He turns to me, as if he knows where my thoughts strayed. He flashes me a perfect smile and grabs my hand.

I smile back, attraction sparking from his gaze.

Across the table, Esper leans forward, reaching for the water pitcher in the center of the table. A memory appears in my mind. *Esper getting stabbed through the stomach, falling off the cliff.* I gasp as I remember. Another memory takes hold. *The Vormr spreading rapidly through the land, plants lying dead in its wake.*

I snap out of the memories. A pulsing headache pounds in my head. The image of Esper's death clings to me.

My friends sit around me, unblinking. Their smiles frozen in place.

"Saline?" I ask.

No response. Just blank stares.

An urgent feeling tells me I need to leave. I stand up abruptly.

Before I can move, a blast of angry air washes over me. I close my eyes against the attack. When I open them, I'm sitting back down at the table.

A feeling of déjà vu sinks over me. But I can't grasp onto any solid thoughts. *What were we just talking about?*

The cheerful voices around me distract my racing thoughts.

Eventually, we agree to turn in for the night. One by one, my friends retreat to their rooms, leaving me alone with my thoughts. Soren snores lightly beside me.

Something tickles the edge of my mind.

Something I'm meant to remember. The more I try to recall it, the further it slips away.

I shake my head and curl up against Soren, letting the warmth of his presence lull me into sleep.

The streetlamp flickers.

Fear grips me as I leap into a boat with Soren and a younger child. Poderosa, my mind whispers.

We cross the water, laughter mixing with the gentle lapping of the waves. The moment shifts, sharpens. We're on the island now, voices turning serious as we speak of the Vormr and my realm.

Then—

A long hallway stretches before me. I step forward—

Nothing.

Darkness.

Flashes of white bones.

A dark and decayed room.

Echoing screams.

"Wake up!"

"Come back to us!"

I jolt awake, sitting up with a gasp, as if reaching the surface of deep water.

Sweat clings to my skin, my heart pounding against my ribs. The dream—no, the memory—tries to hold onto me.

The chamber. I need to get out of here.

I scramble out of bed, throwing on my clothes with shaking hands. The air feels wrong, suffocating. Pressure bears down on my shoulders, any lightness the chamber offered was long gone. I hesitate a moment. My internal thoughts betraying me. *What if I stayed here? I would be happy.*

I shake myself out of my temporary insanity. *No, Adira. This isn't real.*

I enter into the main area and stop. With the fog of the chamber gone, I see what the room really looks like. Skeletons cover the space, shells of the people who have entered before.

Shock and distress cause me to pause at the scene.

One skeleton is holding a cup, frozen mid-toast.

Another is suspended in a crawl, reaching for the door, like they were trying to escape, but didn't make it.

Another is embracing the air, as if they died with the illusion of holding a loved one.

Deep sorrow fills me as I think about all of these people coming to their demise. Unknowingly.

The cruelty shakes me, causing me to sway. *Focus, Adira.*

I race toward the door and shove it open with a grunt.

A hallway stretches before me—long and narrow, *exactly* like in my dream.

I run to the stone door at the other end of it and try to push it. I fall to my knees when a rush of dizziness hits me. My hand lands on a sharp rock and breaks the skin. I hiss. A drop of blood falls onto the cave floor.

The moment it touches the stone— it disappears into it. As if accepting the offering.

A deep groan reverberates through the air.

The door shifts.

Light spills in, blindingly bright.

I squeeze my eyes shut against the sudden glare.

Gasps ring out around me as I stumble forward.

A whisper clings to me as I leave the chamber.

"Come back soon."

I fall forward into the glaring light.

Then—arms wrap around me.

Strong. Familiar.

I collapse into them, relief crashing over me like a tidal wave.

Chapter 23

The air is thick with night, the stars unfamiliar. My body feels like stone, heavy and unresponsive. A dull ache throbs in my skull, and for a moment, I don't know where I am.

My heart pounds, panic taking over. *I have to get out.* I think deliriously.

I force my head to the side, the world spinning with the effort. Concerned blue eyes meet mine. My frantic heartbeat lessens at his gaze, somehow knowing he's the real Soren.

He sits with me in his lap, his arms wrapped securely around me. I push myself up, ignoring the wave of nausea that crashes over me. Poderosa lies sleeping beside a small fire, her tiny body wrapped in a coarse blanket.

"How long was I gone?" I croak, my throat dry and raw.

"You were in the chamber for two days."

My eyes widen.

"I was in there for *two full days?*" My hands shake at the thought.

"Yes." His voice is firm, but there's something tight in it. "I tried to go in after you on the first day, but when I dripped my blood into the bowl, a blast of air knocked me back." His jaw clenches.

"I tried everything, Adira. I would have torn that place apart with my bare hands if I could." He admits wearily, looking down at his hands.

I follow his gaze, gasping at the sight. His knuckles are scraped, angry red lines mar his skin. I gently take his hand in mine.

"What did you do?"

"I tried to get to you." He says simply.

I raise my eyebrows, waiting for him to elaborate.

"When it didn't accept my blood, I found a sharp piece of metal half-buried in the woods. Then, I tried to break my way in. It didn't work, but I wasn't going to give up on you."

I take a slow breath, absorbing the weight of his words. I give his hand a light squeeze of gratitude, then, I let it go.

"Well... I'm here now," I murmur as I shift to sit up fully. My limbs feel sluggish, drained. I barely have the strength to keep myself upright.

The memory of the chamber is still sharp in my mind, an ache settling deep in my bones. An echo of laugh sounds through the trees, I sharply turn my head toward it. Dizziness threatens to overtake me at the swift motion. The forest is still, not even a strong breeze drifts through it.

"Did you hear that?" I ask.

Soren frowns. "No. Hear what?"

I gulp, ignoring the odd feeling.

"Nothing." I correct, forcing a small smile. He looks like he doesn't believe me but doesn't push it.

"It showed me what I wanted most in the world." I told him, hesitating before continuing. "I wanted to stay, Soren. Even when I saw the truth—I almost chose to stay." I admit in a whisper. "My friends had forgiven me. Esper was alive. My magic was full. And... you were there with me."

The haunting voice that followed me out replays in my mind. *Come back soon.* I fight the urge to do just that, the pull of happiness still deeply rooted in me.

Soren's expression softens, his eyes searching mine.

"But it was a false reality," I continue, my voice thick. "I was slowly starving in there without even knowing. As soon as my mind cleared, I saw all the bodies of the people before."

"Soren, there were dozens." I whisper in horror. Their faces lingering in my mind.

"Even now, I can still see them. Smiling. Happy. Frozen in the last moment of their illusion, never realizing they were wasting away."

A shiver runs through me as the realization sinks deeper. If I had been trapped just a little longer... I would have joined them.

I close my eyes against the horrible thought. My mind feeling foggy, unable to fully comprehend my safety.

Soren moves quickly, pulling his pack onto his lap and retrieving a water skin, a small loaf of bread, and some jerky. He presses the food into my hands but doesn't let go.

"Like you said," he murmurs, "you're here now." His voice carries quiet relief. "Now eat all of this." He guides my shaking hands up to my face. My limp arms cry in relief as he carries most of their weight. I nibble on the small loaf of bread, eating slowly. I manage to eat half of the jerky before my stomach stretches, yelling at me to stop. I bring the water skin to my face, hands shaking from the effort. I drink a few sips, soothing my raw throat. Soren watches intently, like he's ready to jump in if I need help.

"You need to rest." He tells me. "We need to leave at first light. I don't want the guards chasing us to get bold enough to come here."

I manage a small smile, my exhaustion bone-deep.

He pulls out a rolled blanket, placing it on the ground beside me. Not bothering to set the bed up closer to the fire, like he knows I wouldn't be able to move the few feet. I lower myself to the ground, placing my head on the makeshift pillow. As sleep pulls at me, I barely register Soren's voice, a whisper meant only for himself.

"I should have stopped you. I should have done something. If you didn't make it out...I don't know what I would have done."

There's something heavy in his words—guilt, regret, fear.

I want to respond, to reassure him. But sleep claims me before I can.

***

A soft rustling wakes me from my lousy sleep. My night filled with recurring nightmares of joyous skeletons.

Except this time, I kept joining them.

I take a deep breath, breathing in the dewy scent of the grass. The smell calming my senses. A small warm body clings to me. I shift my gaze down, seeing Poderosa. *She must have woken up in the night.*

A light rustling sound draws my attention. Turning my gaze toward it, I see Soren packing up our supplies. Something about the sight of him tugs at the back of my mind, an unease I can't quite place.

Soren notices me stirring and asks, "Ready to go?"

I shake off the feeling and nod as I sit up.

"Let's finish this."

Turning to Poderosa, I gently shake her awake. She stirs, rubbing her eyes sleepily. Her expression lights when she sees me awake. She leaps into my arms, hugging me tightly.

She pulls back slightly, looking me in the eyes.

"I tried to talk to you through the door. I thought...I thought maybe you'd forget us."

My stomach clenches.

"I could never forget you, Poderosa. I heard your voices. You and Soren's. You both saved me."

She smiles at that, hugging me again.

Relief passes through me at her smile. *When was the last time I saw her smile?*

I scan the area, noticing smoke in the distance. I freeze.

"Do you see that?" I ask Soren, pointing to the left.

He turns in the direction I'm pointing. Cursing under his breath.

"We aren't the only ones on this island."

"Do you think it's the guards?"

"Probably. I'm not certain anyone else would come here."

"Good point."

We gather our things quickly and set off east toward the mountains of Erontil, careful to avoid the town of Ayward, where the guards will surely be waiting for us.

We melt into the trees. Fatigue pressing in on me rapidly from my still weakened body. A flash of color catches my attention, I twist to the right. A person with copper hair darts between the trees. Esper.

I squeeze my eyes shut. When I open them, she's gone. The forest silent. *I must be hallucinating.* I groan to myself.

I let some magic trickle into my body, clearing my clouded mind and giving me a much needed boost of energy.

As we approach the shore, the silence of the water presses in around me. We hop into the boat, pointing it toward the east, leaving the ruthless island behind. I take a slow breath, letting my thoughts drift to what comes next.

Chapter 24

Three days without any trouble pass before we reach the base of the mountains. *It's about time we got some good fortune.*

While we walk, my mind replays the horrors of the chamber. The vendor's words of warning suddenly becoming clear. Poderosa sticks close to me, like she senses my agitation.

I shake away the thoughts, focusing on the present. My stomach flutters with nerves.

We easily locate the same cave and step inside. A wave of nostalgia washes over me as I move toward the center of the chamber. The lanterns flicker on, blinking gloomily. The air around feeling heavier than before.

Taking a deep breath, I pull out my dagger. Butterflies swarm in my stomach.

This is it. This is the end. All of our problems are finally going to be solved.

Steadying my shaking hand, I press the dagger against my waiting palm. I wince as I reopen the wound from the island, letting my blood drip onto the stone altar.

A gust of wind stirs the air, whipping my hair back. The walls vibrate with unseen energy. The feeling unknown, causing my magic to feel unsettled. A heavy awareness settles over me, like we are being watched.

The air stills and the vibrating energy shifts to a hum, almost creating a quiet song.

Then, two women glide out from behind a pillar. One has long black hair, the other short amber hair, and both radiate an ethereal glow.

The urge to bow overtakes me, I drop to my knees in respect. From the corner of my eye, I see Soren and Poderosa do the same.

"Adira," a voice echoes.

I lift my head up, turning my attention to the dark-haired goddess.

"You have done it. You have passed all the tests and successfully summoned us," she says softly. She motions for us all to stand.

I rise slowly, my wide eyes staying on the beings in front of me.

"Tatsuya?" I breathe out, barely believing it.

She nods with a gentle smile. "Yes, child, it is I." Then she inclines her head toward the other woman. "This is Wilhema Daray."

I stare at the second goddess in awe.

"It's an honor to meet you both."

They return my smile, but Wilhema's expression darkens as she studies me.

"Something is wrong," she murmurs. "A force dims the magic within you. What has happened?"

"There's a Vormr spreading through the land," I explain. "The only way I knew to stop it was to seek your help."

Wilhema nods. "We will check on this."

"What can you—" I start to ask, but before I can finish, both goddesses vanish.

I whip around to face Soren and Poderosa. "Where did they go?"

Before either of them can respond, the goddesses reappear, their expressions grim.

A sense of dread settles in my stomach.

"I found the source of the problem," Tatsuya says tightly, "but I cannot speak of it."

"Why not?" I ask, struggling to keep my frustration in check.

"The three Arae sought me out and revealed a prophecy," she declares.

Wilhema adds, "We cannot interfere when the Arae are directly involved."

Of course they can't. I huff quietly to myself.

"Is there anything you *can* share with me?" I inquire.

Wilhema's eyes narrow from my tone, but then her expression changes to reflect sorrow.

"Yes. I must tell you of the prophecy. The Arae have tasked me to share it with you."

Clearing her throat, she begins:

"The child born from two realms must bond back the creatures that fell. To find out the truth, you must venture back to when divinities were youth. To rebalance what was torn apart, you must forfeit the life of which you hold closest to your heart."

Her voice is grim, and the goddesses give me pitying looks.

A cold sweat breaks out along my back.

"How do you know it's about *me?*" I argue weakly. But even as the words leave my lips, my mind drifts to my childhood. To my mother's constant insistence that I was special, destined for something greater.

Tatsuya sees the realization dawn on my face.

"You already know it is you," she says softly. "I am terribly sorry."

Forfeit the life I hold closest to my heart? My stomach twists violently. *What does that even mean?*

My mother's voice whispers in my mind—'*Be prepared to do whatever is necessary*'—but was this what she meant? The strange lessons she had me study—the afternoons spent learning dead languages, the understanding of dark magic she insisted I was to never use—suddenly make sense.

But still, denial rises up in me.

I swallow hard. "Can you tell me anything else about the prophecy?"

Maybe it's not about me. Maybe they're wrong. I think to myself, latching onto the possibility.

"Unfortunately, that is all I can reveal," Tatsuya says, her tone laced with regret—and finality.

I let out a resigned sigh. *Typical prophecies,* I think. Quickly mulling over it's meaning, I pause on the last part. My eyes darting to the person behind me. *It can't mean him...*

No. That's absurd. I shake away the outlandish thought.

Wilhema steps forward. "We can restore your power."

She reaches out and presses her fingertips to my forehead. A surge of energy floods through me. I inhale sharply, feeling whole again.

"Thank you," I whisper in awe.

Then a thought strikes me—an old friend. "Claude Zephyr!" I blurt out.

The goddesses exchange a glance.

"He was taken," I explain quickly. "Where can we find him?"

Tatsuya closes her eyes. After a few seconds, she opens them and says calmly, "He is safe at home. The guards have no recollection of him being a suspect."

Relief rushes through me. "Thank you."

She smiles sadly. "It is the least I can do."

Her words send a chill through me.

My thoughts turn to my travel companions. *What's one more favor?*

"Can you break a blood oath?" I ask sheepishly.

Wilhema barely hesitates. "Of course."

I explain Soren's situation, and she motions for him to step forward. He hesitates, then approaches slowly, looking wary. Wilhema places a hand on his forehead and murmurs something in an ancient language.

He gasps as the ink on his wrist vanishes. He's free.

"I can't believe it," he breathes. "Tha—thank you." He says in wondrous disbelief. I grin at him.

Wilhema doesn't respond. Instead, she stares at him with an intensity that makes my skin prickle.

"You haven't been truthful," she states.

A heavy silence fills the chamber.

His hands tremble slightly.

"What is she talking about, Soren?" I ask, dread filling me from her tone.

He doesn't answer. His gaze drops to the ground.

Tatsuya turns to me.

"He knew there was a prophecy," Tatsuya says, her voice steady but hard. "And that the Vormr wouldn't be stopped by coming to us."

I gasp and whirl on Soren.

"Is this true?" I demand.

His expression crumbles. "It's true."

My heart shatters at the betrayal.

"I wanted to tell you, but I—"

"I know what you needed," I snap. "You needed to get out of your blood oath."

A horrible thought strikes me. My voice wavers. "Was any of it real?"

"Of course it was, Adira," he says, reaching for my hand.

I jerk away before he can touch me. I take a few steps back, putting distance between him and my shattering heart.

"Do you know how many times I almost died?" I hiss.

A flicker of agony crosses his face. He knows.

His voice cracks. "I had to break it."

Hesitating a moment, he opens his mouth, but nothing comes out. He gasps slightly, gulping down air. I tilt my head curiously, watching his internal battle.

After a moment of struggle, he speaks.

"You don't understand. You weren't the only one who was told things when they were younger." His voice is weighted with guilt.

I grit my teeth. But then, against my better judgment, I give him a chance.

"Okay then. What were you told?" My tone is stiff, unwilling to soften, even as my mind screams desperately. *Please have a good reason.*

Make me believe you. Erase the fact that I feel like a fool for trusting you with my heart.

He hesitates, trying to find the right words.

"I can't tell you," he finally admits. "I was warned against telling anyone."

"Typical," I mutter under my breath.

I turn to the goddesses, hope flaring.

"Can *you* tell me?" I plead.

Tatsuya's gaze softens with sympathy. I already know the answer before she speaks.

"I'm forbidden to say."

I swallow my groan of frustration. *First, they leave me with the burden of the prophecy, now they can't give me any other information?*

A feeling of deep exhaustion encompasses my mind. As if already knowing the despair that will come.

"We must leave now," Tatsuya continues. "We don't want our presence to be known in this realm."

She and Wilhema begin to turn away. But then—Tatsuya freezes. Her gaze shifts past me, her expression shifting from divine composure to shock.

She's staring at Poderosa.

"Poderosa," she whispers. "You've come to me in a dream. I've been waiting for you."

Soren and I both snap our heads toward the girl, momentarily forgetting our argument.

Poderosa steps forward, looking up at Tatsuya with wide eyes.

"Come, child," Tatsuya says. "You must come with me to my land."

"Wait, what? You can't just take her." I stammer out to Tatsuya, terror seizing me at the thought of never seeing Poderosa again.

She calmly turns to me. "She is not meant for your world. She needs to return to her home. She will be safe, I promise."

I swallow past the lump in my throat. Understanding filling me from her words. *I knew she was too different to be from this world.*

Poderosa turns to us, her small hands reaching out to pull us both into a tight embrace. Tears trickle down my face as I hold her close, unwilling to let go but knowing I must.

She places a hand on each of our faces, her touch gentle but grounding. When she speaks, her voice is steady—wiser than the age of her ten years.

"Thank you both," she says. "I will never forget you."

She steps away and takes Tatsuya's hand. Without hesitation, she follows the goddess deeper into the cave, disappearing into the shadows with Wilhema.

And then, I *feel* them vanish. A hollowness takes root in my heart. A large spot that Poderosa filled with her presence.

A deep sadness washes over me, but beneath it is something else— understanding.

Poderosa is where she was always meant to be.

***

Once the silence settles between Soren and I, my anger flares back up. A tremble takes over my body at his betrayal. *How could he do this? If he cared about me at all, he would have told me. Or at least stopped me from doing all those life-threatening tasks.*

My eyes lift to his. His reflecting the sorrow I feel.

Without a word, I turn and storm out of the cave.

He pauses a moment, as if he knows he deserves to be abandoned.

"Adira, wait," Soren calls, his footsteps quick behind me.

"No." I snap, whirling around to face him. "You lied. About everything. I can't trust a word that comes out of your mouth now."

"I had to," he snaps back. His regret turning to frustration.

Running a hand through his hair, he sighs harshly. "You don't understand. I want to tell you."

I let out a bitter laugh. "Convenient that you can't."

His expression darkens, but he doesn't argue. Instead, he asks, "What are we going to do about the prophecy?"

"That's for *me* to worry about," I bite out.

A flash of relief bursts through me. *It can't be about Soren. Not after this.*

I don't give him another chance to respond. With my magic fully restored, I summon a portal to my world, the air pulls at me as if it doesn't want me to leave.

The energy crackles like a storm, churning violently, much like my stomach. I step closer to it, ignoring the fact that it feels colder than it usually does. As if trying to urge me not to go through.

"Please, Adira. Don't leave it like this. I want to help you." He pleads desperately.

Pausing, I glance back at him. Despite my anger, devastation barrels into me. I take in his blue eyes one last time, the ones I came to seek comfort in.

"Goodbye, Soren." My voice is cold, but my heart feels unbearably heavy. "I never want to see you again."

I step forward, and as the portal begins to seal shut behind me, I hear him shouting my name.

Then, silence.

My heart aches painfully from the loss of two souls.

***

As soon as I step through the portal, I'm met with cold steel pressed against my throat.

Welcome home to me.

"You're under arrest for treason, Adira Selcouth."

Instinct kicks in—I reach for my magic, but before I can summon it, a guard senses the shift in energy.

A sharp blow strikes the back of my head.

Darkness swallows me whole.

***

When I wake up, I'm in a cold, dark cell.

Footsteps echo down the corridor, and a familiar, taunting voice follows.

Josephine strolls around the corner, a smirk curling on her lips. "Well, well, look who's back. The little murderer."

I spit at her feet. "The only murderer here is you."

She tilts her head mockingly. "King Elijah and his people don't know that. And since you've been sentenced to death, you won't be able to tell them otherwise." She taps her chin in faux contemplation. Dread stretching through the air as she steps into my cell, leaning in close.

"You're to be hanged at dawn, so who will prove your innocence if you're dead? Hmm... No one will help you now." She speaks softly in my ear. "Personally, I can't wait to see justice be served."

She steps back, smirking at me. "And don't worry, I'll always be around to ensure the *right* people get punished."

As she turns to leave, her laughter bounces off the stone walls, lingering long after she's gone.

I clench my fists, forcing down the wave of panic. I won't die for her crime.

My chest tightens painfully at her words. *Good thing I never needed anyone else.* I think bitterly.

By dawn, I'll be out of here. My mind races with possibilities, lingering on my replenished power.

I just need a plan.

The prophecy has only just begun to unfold.

Acknowledgments

I want to acknowledge my family (includes you, Emma), who let me bounce ideas off them. Thank you for believing in me and listening to all my crazy suggestions.

I also want to thank Books Publishing Company who have been amazing from the start. Thank you to Sebastian & The Editorial Team. As well as Natalia, who helped me every step of the way and answered my millions of questions.

Readers' Note

Welcome to Celestara. I'm thrilled you are here and hope you enjoyed Adira's story. I hope the story offered you the escape you wanted and left you wanting more.

Your presence means so much to me, if you have any questions, thoughts or suggestions, I would love to hear them!

Adira's journey is not over...

For more information, check out my website,

sarakohan.ca

About the Author

Sara Kohan was born and raised in Canada and moved to Italy in 2024. She is an avid reader who enjoys traveling. Sara's love of reading came from her mother and aunt who encouraged her to start reading at a young age. Sara worked at a public library in her town for the entirety of high school. After reading so many books, Sara thought she would give writing one a shot.